The Land of the Shadows

By

Elissa Daye

World Castle Publishing, LLC

This is a work of fiction. Names, characters, places, and incidents are products of the author's imagination or are used fictitiously and are not to be construed as real. Any resemblance to actual events, locations, organizations, or person, living or dead, is entirely coincidental.

WCP

World Castle Publishing, LLC
Pensacola, Florida

Copyright © Elissa Daye 2014
ISBN: 9781629890661
First Edition World Castle Publishing, LLC, March 1, 2014
http://www.worldcastlepublishing.com

Licensing Notes

All rights reserved. No part of this book may be used or reproduced in any manner whatsoever without written permission, except in the case of brief quotations embodied in articles and reviews.

Cover: Lindsay Kendall Graphics
Editor: Maxine Bringenberg

Chapter 1

Lyssa glanced around the clearing, not daring to move too quickly. She shouldn't be out this late at night. The quad was barely lit up, and the shadows covered every inch around her, so she inched forward one step at a time. Lyssa needed to get back to the safety of her dorm room, and she needed to do it now.

A swish of air interrupted the silence behind her. It was not necessary to turn around, for she knew who it was…or rather, what. She grabbed her pentacle between her clasped fingers and took a deep breath. Even though she felt her courage falter, she knew the gods would protect her.

Lyssa walked a few more steps ever so slowly, so that every movement was almost undetectable. The hairs on the back of her neck rose as she closed her eyes and dropped the pentacle. It rested between the rising and falling of her chest as small angry breaths tried to break their way free from her lungs. If it wanted a fight, then so be it. She was fed up with the taunting shape, fed up with the web of darkness that tainted the world around her. When everything in her body told her to flee, she knew it was simply not an option.

Dropping her backpack, she whirled around to face her pursuer. A black shadow stood behind her, a strange black being somewhere between here and there, with no reason or rhyme, just a hollowness that ate up the air around her. It had no discernible facial features, its only human feature a pair of glowing yellow orbs where she assumed its eyes should be. As it moved closer to her, Lyssa knew it was daring her to run.

Gathering her courage, she found her voice. "I will not be threatened any longer." The black being moved closer, floating as if there were no separation between the ground and the air. It reminded her of a ghostly grim from horror stories of long ago, and a shiver ran down her spine. She closed her eyes and concentrated on bringing her energy from within to protect her. Raising her hands, she rubbed them together slowly, picturing the energy that would soon swirl like fire between them. The newly learned skill started to generate heat as she breathed in the air around her and pushed out everything she could into the slowly growing orb of energy in her hands. An electric current started to pick up, and Lyssa took another deep breath to hold it there.

"You need to leave, right now! You're not welcome here!" Part of her might regret banishing it, for she had learned to do no harm, but the desire to live through this moment pushed her forward. She believed in Karma, the magic of redemption and the power of returns, and it sat on her shoulders like some devil vs. angel debate. However, this thing was threatening her, and she had given it plenty of chances to leave while it still could. She had seen it before. It terrorized innocent children at night, and chased people away from places of gathering with feelings of discomfort, ill will, and a gut wrenching need to leave as quickly as possible. It hated happiness and thrived on breaking up the stillness and peace within others. It had visited her the year before, when the difference between life and death had been a mere slice away.

The dark shadow continued to float towards her, and she had no other recourse but to react. Raising her hands, she shouted "Away!" and her hands released the ball of energy. It shot through the air like a speeding bullet, and the bright light singed the darkness in the air around it and smashed into thousands of pieces as it slammed into the shadow. The dark being dissipated into a swirling mist before her, dancing like cigarette smoke in a clear open sky, before it was finally gone.

Now, she walked quickly across the quad, her heartbeat keeping pace with her loud footsteps as they echoed like drumbeats in the silence. Soon, even more would come, and this time there would be a handful to deal with. Lyssa had never retaliated before, and while she felt a slight exhilaration, she dreaded whatever would come next. Now they would be prepared to do more than threaten her space, they would come for everything, but this time she had a plan. By using her inner sight, she would find the entities that were sending out these dastardly minions to do their dirty work and hopefully find the source of the darkness. Unlike the many that were afraid to seek the powers behind these shadows, she would dare them to come, for she did not live in fear anymore. Lyssa had come to this town a year ago, and from the moment she settled into her dorm room, she had felt the presence rooted deeply in the grounds when the light fled and the darkness covered every corner. There was something terribly wrong here, something that she was determined to figure out.

Lyssa remembered the last few years with no fondness. After breaking away from a vicious cycle of family abuse, she had found herself isolated from all her support groups back home, with no friends, no family, no one at all to help her. No one understood her, no one accepted her. No one believed her. Her friends were too uncomfortable with the truths of her past. While she liked to think that her friends had deserted her in her time of need, the truth was she had pushed every single one of them away long before they had gotten the chance. Lyssa hit rock bottom, bruising every inch, every last centimeter of herself in the process.

As she sunk into a deep depression, a desperate despair gripped her as if she were swimming around in a barrel of crude oil, every inch of her being covered in the slimy depression that stained every pore of her skin. Lyssa had always promised herself that she would find a way to get out; that she would move on with her life and move past every sin that had been carved into her soul, every memory that she had meticulously catalogued into a mental filing cabinet of things never to speak of again. She had survived this hellacious life of secrets that had devoured every ounce of her innocence in order to find a freedom she had dreamt about since she was a child. And while she was proud of surviving, proud of how she had escaped a life that had seemed predestined, the moment of her escape was when the darkness had started to appear. That was when the filing cabinet had burst open, and all the sickening memories had come pouring out like a festering wound that had never healed, a wound so deep and infected that no simple Band-Aid would ever work to conceal the pain oozing out of it.

Lyssa had barely noticed it, this shadow of cold darkness. It had lingered so close that she had only to reach out a finger to feel its presence. It was the shadow, the shadow that was cold yet familiar to her at the same time, for she had lived a lifetime surviving the evil emanating from it. The being had seemed to gaze at her from the window, almost as if to ask her to embrace her malcontent. Like a parasite, it had watched her from outside her room, growing larger every time it siphoned more life and joy out of her from a distance.

Suddenly, she had discounted everything she had done to get where she was; the strength that she'd kept hidden from the rest of the world, and all the good things that she had transplanted into her life. The darkness came for her and built its tomb around her with icy talons that shook her to the very core. She had never thought of ending everything before then. Her plan had been to survive, to get away from her father's corrupted grasping hands before he took everything she had left to give to the world.

When the black void came, so had the whispering voices, voices that she had never heard before that moment. They brought volatile emotions that made her tremble like a leaf on the wind. "Just end it. End it now. Who will care? Who will miss you?" When she found strength to carry her through those restless nights, the voices found another weakness. They soon began to blame her for everything that had gone wrong in the lives of those she cared about the most. Those attacks had bitten at her like mosquitoes, at first with timid suckles at the flesh of her guilt, then strong gasping gulps that had devoured every inch of her courage. "End it. You deserve to die. Look at what you've done to your family. It's all your fault. You deserved it. End it. Then no one will be hurting anymore."

Before long, she had lost herself to the moment when the voices got too strong to ignore. "You don't have anyone. No one wants you. No one loves you. They never did." The message had repeated itself over and over again. She remembered the knife that she had used to carve a pumpkin the night before…it glistened from across the room as the candlelight cast its light around it. Suddenly, the temptation to pick it up and slash had risen so close to the surface of her mind that she had crossed the distance of the room and picked it up without a thought. Standing there in the stillness with the knife shaking in her hand, she had held it against her wrist. That was when she had heard a woman's voice interrupt the record, and its message started to skip like a pebble across a pond.

"The world would be a much sadder place without you."

Lyssa had turned to the sound and seen a spirit standing beside her. Her long brown cascading curls were swept up into a Grecian coronet. She wore a white gown that looked like something from a Greek mythology book that she had read in high school. Lyssa had never seen her before, yet her presence had seemed vaguely familiar.

The knife had clattered as it fell to the floor at her feet, leaving Lyssa staring in awe at the spirit before her. "Why would anyone be sad that I was no longer here? No one needs me anyway."

"It is difficult for them to reach you now, for they have not traveled the roads you have. In time, your friends will understand. They need time to adapt. You must fight the darkness that tries to control your thoughts."

"What are they?" Lyssa had asked her.

"You must discover that for yourself. Until you do, you must remember that you have a greater purpose than this thing can ever touch." The spirit gestured to the being floating outside her window. "You have to keep fighting, keep believing, keep living."

When Lyssa had tried to ask her more, the spirit had already disappeared. It wasn't until later that she learned that the spirit, Jephilia, was her spirit guide. The witty being had a way of disappearing before answering her questions in detail. When Jephilia wasn't shocking her sides with energy jolts to get her attention, she was dropping messages that only a saint could interpret. From that moment, Lyssa had been able to break through the thoughts that had lived like a parasite in her brain for the past year, and she began to work on inner peace to build a barrier that the darkness could not touch.

Chapter 2

When she finally reached her dorm, she knocked on Jackson's door. After a year of begging him to leave his college in Utah, he had come back home to Illinois, and now lived right down the hall from her. They clicked in ways no one in this world could ever understand—in ways that confounded both of them from time to time—with an immeasurable bond that seemed to transcend time and space. They had been to hell and back together, and the hand basket they had traveled in had been worn and tattered along the way, but with love and nurturing, it was still intact. Jackson had been a lifeline in a time of darkness.

"What's with that cold air?" He opened the door, and his hazel eyes darted to the hallway. It never failed to amaze her how tall he was compared to her average stature, and how his handsome features were always enhanced by the spiky brown hair with his blond and red highlights. Sometimes, she wondered if his magical abilities allowed him to roll out of bed without a hair out of place, for he made his appearance seem effortless.

"It was following me again, so I took care of it. Now they're really pissed."

"Come inside," he said quickly, closing the door behind him. "I'll light some candles and burn some incense right away."

"I'll make an energy barrier. They're coming, and we need to protect ourselves. We can't let them find us." Lyssa took her wand out of her backpack and started to draw a protective circle around them, calling silently to each of the four corners to protect them from the darkness outside.

"What are they going to do?" Jackson asked her as he lit the last candle for spirit to protect them.

"I don't know, but I'm tired of running. There are enough of us on this campus to do something about those things out there. First, we need to find out where they're coming from." Looking through her bag of oddities, she let out a sigh of relief when she found the feather from one of the large crows that spent a lot of time outside her window. Lyssa had considered the possibility that this particular bird was one of her totem animals, so she had picked up the feather to preserve the link that she had felt to him. When she had first channeled with him, she knew at once that she was right. From that moment on, the black bird seemed to follow her everywhere, and she had taken to calling him Thor.

Lyssa placed the feather in the middle of their circle and pondered how she could work with her totem to find this evil presence. "Keep an eye out. I'm going in." She sat down and crossed her legs in front of her. Picking up the feather from the floor, she held it in her right hand, and then grounded herself by breathing in the energy around her until she could see the rainbow of energy flowing from the top of her head to the bottom of her feet. Lyssa called out to the bird in an ethereal voice that was in between planes of existence. "Thor, brother bird, let me see what you see. Let your eyes be my eyes. Show me where they are."

As the bird took flight, she could only see through its eyes. It felt as if she were wearing blinders that blocked out everything except what she could see in the space on her forehead between her two eyes, right where the axis of the third eye was located. He flew away from the college campus and down the main street that connected the two sister cities. Then the bird soared over the movie theater, the grocery store, and past the hospital. Soon, he was crossing over downtown to where the old abandoned factory buildings were located. When he reached one of these buildings, Thor perched on a windowsill on the fifth floor.

The building was like any other abandoned building. The windows were filmy; some broken, some boarded. This window was clouded over, making it hard to see the people inside, but it was easy to feel the darkness that her totem felt. The air was thick, making it hard to breathe. The disturbing blackness was ebbing around her like the pulse of a migraine at the front of her temples. After a few moments, the bird trained its eyes on the occupants of the room.

A small murmuring of collective voices came from inside. Five people stood near the flames of a small fire, chanting words that were indecipherable to the outside world. As the chanting got louder, the flames rose higher from the old oil barrel, so high that the flames seemed to leap into the air and live separately from their earthly container. They took the shape of the shadows, much like the shadow she had seen earlier this evening. It seemed to turn with haunting accuracy as it looked directly to where Thor was perched outside. Instantaneously, she felt the air being sucked out of her lungs, and the sight that her totem spirit had provided her was quickly deflected. She dropped the feather and gasped, "They're on to me. Quick, send the guardians to erase our location before we're found."

Jackson sent guardians of each corner...North, East, South and West. They needed protection from the minions that were sure to find them if they did not act quickly. While he summoned the guardians, she asked her spirit guides to push out any unwelcome guests from their dorm as they waited in silence.

The phone rang, and Jackson picked it up before the second ring. "Hello?"

"What the hell did you do?" Lana accused through the phone.

"What do you mean?" Jackson asked quietly.

"Have you seen the shadows outside? They're all circling the campus right now, you moron! Tell me you didn't try to find them?"

"We may have tried to find them. But, we can't worry about that right now. We've sent out the guardians to mask our location."

"I'm on my way." Lana's annoyance was clear even from across the room.

"Oh lord, here we go!" Lyssa sighed outwardly. "She'll bring her whole coven with her before long. We don't need that attention here."

"Give her some credit, Lyssa. She won't take any unnecessary risks."

After ten minutes, there was a knock on the door. Jackson opened it up to find a man that neither one of them had seen before. "You two, come with me right away." His voice was as commanding as his sudden presence.

"Who the hell are you?" Lyssa put her hand on the phone, ready to dial for help.

"It doesn't matter at the moment. We need to get you out of here. Right now. It's for your own good. Think of it as a witness protection situation." His face was shadowed and hard to read. He pulled out his wand and fired a bolt into the hallway behind him. Jackson and Lyssa both pulled out their wands and jumped to the door to peer outside. There were shadows closing in on them, and there was no escape.

"Grab my hand if you want to live!"

They quickly shot glances at each other, knowing that there was only one option, and it was not a choice they would normally take. They would have to trust this stranger and put their hope for survival out to the universe. Lyssa closed her eyes as she grabbed his hand, half expecting to be devoured by the shadows swirling right behind them. There was a static electricity pop and then a whoosh of air around them.

Elissa Daye

Chapter 3

When she opened her eyes they were in a dark room, and her eyes were adjusting horribly to it. "Jackson, where are you?"

"Here, Lyssa. You okay?" he asked her quickly.

"Yes. You?"

"I seem to be intact," he replied.

"Oh, how touching," came a sarcastic reply.

"Lana?" she asked.

"Yes dearie. I'm here, too. He saved me just before he came to you."

Lyssa imagined the sarcastic sway of her golden curls. The petite blonde would never let her live this one down. "Who? And exactly where is he?"

"Light!" whispered a voice near her, and the room was filled with light. The man was holding up his wand like a flashlight that brightly lit up the spaces around them.

"Show off," Jackson mumbled.

"Who the hell are you?" Lyssa demanded. You didn't just whisk someone away and not expect to answer questions. He could be a lunatic for all she knew, which reflected poorly on her judgment. She should know better than to just go off willy-nilly like that.

"Wrong question, but I'll be happy to answer the right one."

"You see, Lyssa, I already tried that route. He seems to think that we don't live in a day and age where stranger danger matters anymore." Lana rolled her eyes to emphasize her sarcasm.

"And yet you came with me anyway," he shot right back at her.

Lyssa took a closer look at the man, since she really did not have the chance earlier. He appeared to be in his early thirties. His black hair was trimmed in a short, well-tailored style, but his face was not as cleanly kept. He looked as if he had not shaved his face in a while, as the five o'clock shadow had been multiplied by days. He was dressed totally in black, from his v-neck cotton t-shirt down to the jeans that were fitted tightly around his black steel-toed boots. A tattooed roman numeral four was etched in his right forearm. There was a pentacle peeking out from underneath his shirt, and he was glancing at her with a knowing smile.

"Fine, we'll do this the hard way," Lyssa said with determination. She closed her eyes and took a deep breath, opened her eyes, and looked at him square in the face. She imagined spidery silk weaving its way from within her temple and working its way slowly through the air. While Lyssa waited for her mind to connect with his, his smirk sent a challenge to her. He had no idea how adept she was at reading minds, so getting into his thoughts should be easier than he expected. With every ounce of her will power she pushed against the resistance, only for it to rebound back at her from his silent spell of protection, causing her to stumble back a few steps. Lyssa glared at him as her chin jutted out rebelliously.

"Ah-ah-ah!" He clicked his tongue to the roof of his mouth. "Come now, Lyssa, you can do better than that.

Perhaps you should go back to figuring out what the right question is."

"Fine, Julius, why are we here?" she asked him with a tilt of her head and an eyebrow risen in challenge.

"Very good, Lyssa. Now if only Logan would remember to stand further away from this room, you would still be guessing." A younger man stepped into the room from the hallway. He looked down at the ground and clasped his hands in front of him.

"It's not like baiting them is going to help the situation," mumbled Logan. His brown hair framed his face like an old-fashioned barbershop bowl cut. While never in fashion back in the day, apparently now it was very sheik, due to some new singing pipsqueak all the preteens followed around like the new antichrist. Was it some kind of chipmunk, or was it a beaver?

She looked back at Julius and raised her wand to show she meant business. "I'm not afraid of you. Now tell me why we are here."

"I can take you back if you like," he suggested with a subtle grin on his face.

"Not the point. Answer my question!"

"My, my. She sure is a feisty one," a female voice called through the doorway. A very pale woman with long red hair sauntered into the room. She put her hand on Julius's shoulder and peered down at Lyssa with more hostility than she deserved. "This is the girl you were talking about? She's extremely rash and unrefined." The redhead looked at him in disbelief.

"Serena, quiet. We'll discuss that later." Julius pulled her arm off his shoulder and walked to the window that was now visible through his wand light.

It was easy to see by the way she tossed her hair and crossed her arms that Serena was feeling snubbed by Julius. The quiet tap of her foot, clad in black stiletto boots, beat out her irritation on the floor. Part of Lyssa wondered what she had to do with any of this, but the majority of her thoughts were jumbled up right now. "Why are we here? Where are we? And why the hell can't someone turn on a real light?"

"Because the shadows will find you," answered Logan. When Julius looked at him pointedly, he raised his arms. "What? You think it's more helpful if she doesn't know about the shadows? You can't just whisk these people away without telling them about the danger they were in."

"Danger?" Lyssa laughed. Who did these people think they were? She would have found a way out of that situation. It might have taken longer, but she would have figured it out. "We would've handled it."

"Well, she sure does think a lot of herself." Serena's saucy voice felt like fingernails on chalkboards. No, actually, it was the heated way that Serena looked at her that made her feel that way.

"Forget you." She stood up and nodded her head at Jackson. "Let's get out of here. We have to stop those things."

"Lyssa, wait." Lana looked at her seriously. "You may think you can take on the world, but you didn't see how many of those things were coming this time. There's no way we were getting out alive. We've played with fire long enough."

"Take them to the library," Julius commanded. He still had not turned away from the window. It was as if he was tracking something outside the room, but nothing could be seen in the darkness outside.

They waited in the library for what seemed like an hour, but without a clock on the wall, it was hard to tell. Lyssa heard the raised voices of Julius and Serena from upstairs. Apparently, they disagreed about something. All she could hear was the word "guardian" and "watch tower." Just when she was going to suggest they leave, Julius entered the library, followed by a very disgruntled Serena.

"So?" Lyssa couldn't help raising her eyebrows questioningly at Julius while she let the word echo slowly around them. He seemed to be the leader of this group. Perhaps she would have to play nice if they were going to leave on a peaceful note.

Julius inhaled deeply and let out a long sigh. "We would have met eventually. Later would have been better than sooner. You're just not ready yet."

Jackson beat her to the punch line this time. "Who is not ready? And ready for what?"

Lyssa looked over at Jackson and nodded her head. "That's exactly what I want to know too."

"Tell them, Julius. It's too late to send them back." Logan gestured to Julius while pushing his hair away from his face. "You have to tell them."

"Oh good lord. I'll tell them then." Serena eyed her speculatively. "We are the Guardians of the Watch Tower."

"Which one?" Lyssa asked them cautiously. She had never met a guardian before, and she had assumed that they were magical entities that represented each magical element.

"Not *those* watch towers," Julius breathed out in annoyance, his dark eyebrows arched severely as if to make his point.

"Wow, calm down." She was getting tired of him looking like he was ready to snap. They may have gone a little overboard tonight, but there was no reason to treat them with hostility.

"We are Guardians of The Watch Tower, the only one that keeps a constant vigil out in the darkness. We are currently focusing our attention on the Land of the Shadows."

"Is that where they come from?" Now he had her full attention, for Lyssa wanted to know where these shadows originated. How did they get formed? Who created them? How could they defeat them? Why had they chosen this town? People were dying more mysteriously around there every day.

"The Land of the Shadows is below us, wherever we walk," Logan interrupted.

"So they come from Hell?" Jackson pursed his lips speculatively.

"If you believe in Hell," Julius answered. "What some call Hell, we call the Land of the Shadows. Everything dark comes from beneath the Earth, where the light never reaches."

"Great, all these years I've spent not believing in the existence of Hell, and here you go telling me that there is one." Lana shook her head disbelievingly.

"I don't think he said that. I think he is saying that darkness exists there, not the infernal blazes we're often told about. So if that is the case, how are they surviving above ground? Where are they coming out?" Lyssa looked at Julius questioningly.

"See, I told you she's the one," Logan said quietly. He stood against the wall with his hands in his pockets.

"Excuse me? I'm what one?" What in the world was he talking about? Why was she being mentioned again? "Look, I didn't mean to cause a problem. I just want to find out why they are destroying the people in my town. Do you know have many suicides we had last year? Suicides are almost up into the hundreds now. I know these things are causing it. They're probably doing this in other places too."

"I'm not surprised that you have made the connection. It's true, the shadows feed upon weaker spirits. They are finding other means to do this as well. The Craven are responsible for this. But that is a long story." Julius waved his hand in front of him.

"You dodged my question yet again. What do you want with me? What about my friends?" Lyssa looked at Lana and Jackson. Were they in trouble? If this was something she brought upon her friends, she would never forgive herself.

"You are the missing guardian." It was one statement. One simple statement from Julius, and the room was deadly silent. It was as if the world stopped turning while they looked at each other questioningly.

"Me? Or all of us?" Lyssa knew Lana and Jackson must also be wondering.

"He said guardian, not guardians. That implies one," Lana repeated.

She let it sink in. This man was calling her a lost guardian. Lyssa had no idea what that was supposed to mean. What did a guardian do? Would she have to leave behind her friends, and if so, why would she even want to do that?

"That is correct. Lyssa, you are a lost Guardian of the Watch Tower. You are young, impetuous perhaps, but there is no denying you have the intuition to be great."

Lyssa giggled. No one had ever referred to her as great before. She felt like a striped tiger ready to eat a great big bowl of corn flakes. "Wow, you're funny. All right, where's the camera? Are you punking me?"

"Are you taking us back now?" Lana asked him. "I assume she'll stay here. But what about us?"

"What? Why the hell would I stay here?"

"It's your destiny," answered Logan.

"Are you for real?" She looked at Jackson, who looked like he was turning hot under the collar. "If you think I'm leaving her behind, you must be on crack." He crossed his arms and tapped his foot defiantly.

"And if you make him go, I will find a way to follow." Destiny? Who the heck believed in destiny these days?

"Non-negotiable."

"Fine. Let's go then, shall we?" Lyssa pointed to the door behind them and grabbed Jackson's arm. When they reached the doorway, Lyssa was surprised to hear Serena clearing her voice, and a small "Ow!" echoed around them.

"All right. Fine. You can both stay, but the witch goes."

"Wow, I do have a name you know. The witch…real classy people you have here. Might as well have said 'the dumb blonde.'" Lana rolled her eyes.

Julius interrupted her small tirade. "It is safe for you to return now. The shadows are gone."

"Fine. I'm ready to go any time you are." Lyssa was so ready to be out of there. They were all speaking crazy talk, and she did not have to stay there and listen to it.

"You stay."

"I'm sorry, did I sign my name on the dotted line somewhere? What incentive do I have to stay here?"

"Do you want to rid the world of the shadows?" The redhead crossed her arms before her and tilted her head in the air.

Lyssa was on her way out the door when Jackson answered "Yes, we do." Jackson pulled on her arm and raised his eyebrows at her.

"Dammit. Fine. We stay." Lyssa crinkled her nose at Jackson and sniffed in a huff. She hated when he stared at her like that. Usually it meant he was right, and somehow she was horribly wrong. Right now she had no idea how she was in the wrong, but she had learned to trust his instincts.

"It's settled then. Until it is safe for you both to return, you will stay here." Julius reached out his arm to Lana. Lana smiled softly at them before reaching out to him. Lana and Julius were gone faster than a heartbeat.

Lyssa stood there in shock. Everything she had come to understand about the world around her was somehow tilted, and she was left there in the silence trying to figure out what she was going to do. The smug look on Serena's face was more than she could take, a look so filled with malice that something snapped inside her. She stepped towards her to knock the smile from her face, but was held back by Jackson.

"Don't let her get to you, Lyssa. She's not worth it, trust me." Logan turned toward her, and she ducked her head. Lyssa did not want him to see the angry tear that was trying to make its way from her eyes. If she knew how to leave this place, she would have already been gone, but she was stuck inside this dark room and starting to feel like a raccoon trapped inside a cage for the second time in her life. It would be so easy to lash out at the world around her and to tear her claws into anything she could get a hold of as she hissed in outrage, but the fact of the matter was that these people could have powers that were infinitely stronger than any she possessed. What real action could she possibly take? The only solace she had was that Jackson was there beside her.

Elissa Daye

Chapter 4

As she stood there by the fireplace, her insides churned to the slow tick of the clock on the mantle as helplessness saturated the silence. She had promised herself that she would never feel that way again, and yet there she was, standing with a nervous sweat running down her forehead. At least that Serena was not there to see it. Lyssa was still trying to figure out what animal crawled up her ass, for she had never met her before. That woman would never see an inch of weakness, never crack the mask that she displayed to the world.

As the time continued to pass, it was even clearer that Julius had not yet returned. This bothered her. What if something had happened in transit? Did the shadows find them? Lyssa could only hope that Lana would be safe back on campus. She would have requested that her friend stay there as well, but Lyssa knew that Lana would never leave her coven behind. Lana was very devoted to her group and would do everything in her power to protect them.

Lyssa could not believe everything had happened so quickly. One moment she and Jackson were sitting inside his room, and the next they were in some bizarre twist of fate. It was an unbelievably unrealistic situation, but when magic was involved, perhaps that was the only way reality spun. It was bad form to tell someone they were chosen for a higher purpose and then rip them away from everything they'd ever known. At least that was what it seemed like. Not very much detail or explanation had been given yet, and all Lyssa could do was sit and stew.

How could she possibly have been chosen for a higher purpose? Lyssa was barely treading water most days. There was so much turmoil and angst inside her. Did they really expect her to be able to contribute anything meaningful? It had never occurred to her that the spiritual beliefs that she had discovered in college were actually a calling in life; a past time maybe, but not a calling. At first, this spirituality was an escape route. While attempting to leave the darkness of her past where it belonged, Lyssa had disappeared completely into this new magical world…not your every day smoke and mirrors kind of magic. There was no sleight of hand…this really existed.

She had attended a Samhain ritual as Lana's guest her first year of college. She was always up for new things. At first, she had absolutely no idea why she had agreed to go. Five minutes into the ritual, she had seen with her own eyes that the magic was real. When Lyssa had observed the orbs of light surrounding the circle, she had felt the bizarre lack of air within it, as outside of the circle they had been surrounded by swaying leaves. The silence, while eerie at times, was a potent messenger that carried infinitely more wisdom in its wake.

Soon after the ritual, she had found herself pouring into new age books, asking questions of other practitioners, and performing daily meditations to bring her closer to a higher power. Then Lyssa found herself becoming in tune with all of nature's energy. It drowned out the noise and let her simply be one with the world around her. It was like a lifeboat had been thrown to her with a new hope for the future, and yet she still could not figure out why it had chosen her.

Today felt just like that first time. There was something attractive to being something more than she ever imagined she could be, to being something more than she was…but what exactly was that? Did she really know what the Watch Tower was? Who were these guardians? Where did they go when they were not there? And where in the world was the Watch Tower? There were so many questions that she did not have the answer to, and it bothered her that they had already left her feeling cornered, left her feeling completely lost and inept, while keeping her trapped within their realm, even with Jackson at her side.

She heard a swish of air and saw the candles flicker around her. Lyssa turned around slowly, even though she knew that Julius had returned. "You're back." It was difficult not to react to the emotions bubbling beneath the surface, hence the flat sound of her voice. Part of her would have been thrilled to be a part of something bigger, but it was the part that was left behind that called to her.

"You're upset."

"Really Sherlock? What made you think that?" She crossed her arms in front of her and could feel her chin jut out. It always did that when she was moody.

"In time, it will pass." He shrugged her off easily, as if he were hardened to her situation.

"No, it won't. Jackson's my family. He's all I have left and you wanted to rip him away from me. You underestimate that bond."

"Lyssa, he let me stay. We walk this path together." Jackson put a hand on her arm.

"Don't you get it? I've spent my entire life being told what to do, with very few choices, no way out." Lyssa could feel the heat filling her cheeks.

"Lyssa, he never said we didn't have choices. Let the poor man speak."

"Whose side are you on, Jackson?" Lyssa turned to Jackson, almost ready to speak her mind, when another voice interrupted the conversation.

"Was it really so long ago that you've forgotten what it's like, Julius? Please, forgive me for intruding. I didn't mean to be late."

He had short brown hair clipped close on the sides, with spiky curls on the top. It was hard to tell the color of his eyes from her position, but thick eyelashes curled secretively around them. His tall body was covered in black from the tight fitting t-shirt that molded close to his upper torso, to the black denim jeans that were not nearly tight enough. From what Lyssa could see, he was simply dazzling, a rock star to be admired from afar and ravished secretly in any girl's fantasies. And he seemed very familiar to her.

Lyssa tried to hide behind her curiosity, because what she was feeling was certainly more than that. His mere presence took her breath away, for there was something very intriguing about him that called to a hidden part of her. "And you are?" She could almost feel the tint of a blush rising in her cheeks.

"Hunter, at your service."

As he moved closer, his eyes roamed over her far longer than she expected. What Lyssa wouldn't give to melt into their smoky blue depths. She pursed her lips and did her best to hide behind her attitude, to push bravado out to the people around her, but for some reason her words had suddenly left her. Lyssa could pinpoint the very moment she'd become mute…it was when the first words left his mouth. While she was still upset about being ripped away from her life, there could still be an upside for this situation, for her soul seemed to beckon her closer to him. A thrill ran through her body, almost as if to say "something wicked this way comes." What Lyssa wouldn't do with a man as hot as that if given the chance. "Well, Hunter, perhaps you can tell your friend here that he should explain more about the Watch Tower, and exactly what it is that he wants from me—er, us. I promise you, if we don't get answers, we will find a way to get out of here."

From the way that Julius looked at Hunter, she could tell right away that they were having some kind of mental conversation. If she didn't know better, she would say they were actually arguing, as Hunter's naturally angled brows arched further. Lyssa waited as they continued their silent debate and started to walk to the window.

"Step away from the window," ordered Julius quickly.

It was then that she saw what Julius had been trying to protect her from. Outside, the shadows were slowly seeping from the ground. The rising forms were looking right at her, and it was clear that they had been sent to find her. "Why are they still looking for me?"

"Because you are the key." Hunter grabbed her elbow and urged her away from the windowpanes. "I know you don't trust us, but please, there's very little time before they burst through those walls. We have to get you out of here."

"You already rescued us once today; where in the world are you taking us now?" The way that his eyebrows dropped was a true indicator that she was not scoring any points right now. Lyssa hadn't meant to snap at Hunter, but even the slight touch of his hand on her arm made her flush in ways she could not explain. Not that it mattered, for he was amazingly attractive, and...well...she was just her, tall enough, yet not really skinny enough to pull it off. Lyssa had long brown hair that she often wished had a more lively color to it. Then there was her absolutely large feet, covered in shoes that looked much like small boats. She often wondered if she could walk on water with the gargantuan monstrosities, but had never tested out the theory. If there was anything to like about herself, besides her ability to overcome seriously daunting challenges, it was her eyes. They were the one thing she had never wanted to change. Blue simply could not define them. They were otherworldly, like the calm waves of a deserted beach, so endless and blue you could get lost in them. Lyssa had no idea where she'd gotten them....no one else in her family seemed to have the same shade.

"We really don't have time for this." Julius grabbed her arm, breaking her reverie, and she felt the world go like a Tilt-A-Whirl once more as they were once again speeding through the air. Any words she wanted to utter were hard to get past her teeth, as this unfashionable traveling made them clench tightly together against the rush of wind. This journey seemed to take a lot longer than before, and soon she had no idea where one moment started and the other ended. It seemed to take forever to get to their destination.

"Really, is that necessary?" She scowled deeply at Julius as they finally arrived. If ever there were a man she wanted to strangle, it would definitely be him. He was a pompous know-it-all who seemed to dictate to everyone around him.

"Yes, I can tell how much you detest me. I'm an acquired taste, I assure you." His slight grin reminded her that he had been kinder to her earlier, and she should practice a little patience. If he kept zooming her from one place to another, there was no way she would make it back home. Lyssa could not even begin to guess where they were now.

"I doubt it," coughed Jackson into his hand.

She sighed deeply. "Fine. I'm sorry, Julius. Cut me some slack though."

"I know you want answers. I promise to give them to you both. I just need to check on a few things first. Please make yourself at home."

Jackson's eyebrows furrowed. "What about...?"

"The shadows? Don't worry, Jackson. They can't find you here." With a quick pop of air he disappeared.

She looked around her. The room was actually quite large. From the antique trim around the floors and ceilings, she appeared to be in the parlor of an older Victorian house. Near the window was a round table that was draped in a deep red velvet. On top of the table were different gemstones that glowed eerily in the night. The small fire burning in the fireplace to her right crackled, and on its mantle a small ball of light glowed under a glass dome. Lyssa had no idea what was inside, but for some reason, she knew it was not to be touched. In the middle of the room was a large, overstuffed burgundy sofa that was draped with an old, intricately crocheted afghan. This house had history and a character that was rich and palpable, the kind of house that Lyssa had always wanted to own.

Lyssa walked over to the windows that were protected by curtains that reached from the ceiling to the floor. The attractive burgundy taffeta made it look like ripples of dark water flowed within its folds. She moved aside the curtains, and when she looked out, she was actually speechless. She had expected to see a street lined with old historic houses, perhaps a few mature oak trees, but that was not the sight that greeted her. Instead, all she saw was a dark sky lined with stars. She attempted to look down from the window and saw no earth beneath her. From every angle, it appeared as if the house was surrounded by nothingness. While she was standing on a wooden floor inside this house, there was emptiness below it. They were literally in outer space.

The realization that things were more difficult than she had first imagined hit her so fast, her head started to spin. She walked ever so slowly to the couch and let herself slide down into its cushions. Her head began to throb painfully as she took even breaths to calm herself. Perhaps it was true that if the shadows came from the land below her feet, then being in a house with no land underneath could in fact mean that the inhabitants of the house were safer here. Lyssa didn't feel safe though. Surrounded by strange people, she was away from the life that she had started to build for herself. She had been studying to be a teacher, and had thought that was what she was meant to do. However, perhaps her boredom in clinical studies should have been a warning that she was supposed to do something else with her life. Perhaps, in a way, this would be saving her from a life saturated with angry parents, unsupportive administrators, and children with problems she would never be able to solve.

When she glanced at her wrist, her watch now read midnight. They had been away from her dorm for hours now. Lyssa wondered what Lana might be doing right now, and every bone in her body hoped that she was safe. Would the shadow people come back for her? Was she okay? There had to be some way to know she was all right. Jackson plopped down next to her, and they sat in silence until Julius returned and escorted them to guest rooms to rest.

Chapter 5

It was a bizarre thing, to wake up in a house filled with sunlight when she was not quite sure if the sun could actually reach her. Lyssa still had no idea where she was or how exactly this place was even possible. Was she actually in outer space? If she opened the window, would the lack of air outside suck her brains out of her ears?

Lyssa sat up in bed and shook the sleep from her head. Considering the events of the night, she had actually slept quite well. When Julius had escorted her and Jackson to guest rooms upstairs, they had called it a night. While she expected her intuition to guide her while she slept, she was surprised that for once, her dreams were meaningless.

Lyssa sat down at the vanity dresser on the other end of the room and looked in the mirror. Her hair was such a mess. Running her fingers through it, she attempted to straighten up some of the unwieldy locks that framed her face. She pulled a hair tie out of her back pocket and worked on pulling the mess out of her face. It was no grand coiffeur, but it would have to do.

Opening the door, she entered the hallway. It was dark last night when they had walked upstairs, so she was not exactly sure where she was going, but if she took the stairs down, she would run into someone else eventually. As she walked down the steps, she could not help but notice the magnificent woodworking. The dark wood contrasted deeply with the small carpet running down the steps. The walls were lined with antique frames of faces that looked extremely dated for the current time, almost as if the original inhabitants of the house had left them behind. The floral print wallpaper was starting to fade with age, and while it was probably beautiful in its prime, it was starting to crackle at the seams.

When she reached the bottom of the stairs, she found the entrance to the parlor. Since this was the place that Julius had brought her to first, she figured she should make herself at home there.

As she sat down on the couch, Lyssa took a personal assessment. No worse for the wear at the moment...her nerves were intact. No one seemed to be stirring at all, so Lyssa decided to do some meditation to clear any negative energy within her. Anger often came too easily to her, and her emotions seemed too volatile to control, but they were so much a part of her that it was hard to let them go.

She took in a deep breath and curled her toes underneath her legs. Closing her eyes, she let the quiet take her away. Lyssa must have been there for a good half hour, glued to the sofa like a stone statue, before she heard her voice.

"You must let go of your past."

"Jephilia. My past defines me. I can't just let it go. It doesn't work that way. And if you mean let go of Jackson, you are seriously mistaken if you think that is ever going to happen."

"Lyssa, listen closely. He will be there whenever you need him, but you can't let him hold you back."

"Let me guess...I'm destined for greatness." If her eyes had been open, they would have rolled to the ceiling.

"You are destined for whatever you decide. No one can make you do. No one can make you be. You simply are. Follow or don't. The path has always been yours to take."

"I didn't have a choice last night. No one even bothered to listen to me."

"If they had, would you even have considered the possibilities they presented?"

Lyssa sighed slowly. Jephilia was not one to drag out her conversations with her. Most of the time, her spirit guide was quite happy to say very little. She interfered only when she needed her most, and today Jephilia clearly thought she needed to jump into the middle of everything. She looked at the Grecian girl and shook her head. "You're right. I would've discounted what they had to say. I'm not one to trust easily. Look how long it took me to let you speak with me."

Jephilia's skirt fluttered in the air around her. Her guide made an audible chuckle that was so unlike the serious guide she normally portrayed. "Keep your mind open and look deeper with your eyes."

Lyssa was not surprised when she quickly disappeared. Well, at least she was not as cryptic with her messages today. That was a bonus. When she heard a shuffling of feet, she looked up to see Hunter and Julius entering the parlor. Lyssa started to open her mouth, but was at a loss for words. She was still confused about everything that had just happened, and not at all sure that she would continue forward with civil thoughts in her head.

Julius raised his hand to wave her off. "I have something to show you. Please come with me."

"Where is Jackson?"

"He's already there. Follow me, please."

Lyssa thought to deny his request for a moment, but the warm smile that Julius actually offered this time threw her off enough to shake away her hesitation. She nodded at him and rose from the sofa. Her footsteps echoed theirs as she followed them out of the room into what appeared to be a dining room. It also exuded the essence of a proper Victorian house, from the top of the wood molded ceiling to the wooden floors covered in bold woven rugs; there were even built in china cabinets and retractable pocket doors. Lyssa was so caught up in the ambience that she did not notice the guest at the table.

"Oh my gosh!" Lyssa could not help the squeal that left her mouth so easily. Lana was sitting at the table next to Jackson, eating a piece of toast that almost wedged itself in her throat when Lyssa threw herself at her. "I thought I'd never get to see you again."

Jackson looked at her and chuckled. "She's only been gone for one night."

"I know, and we always thought you were the drama queen." Lana gestured to Jackson.

"Oh, stop it. I'm just glad to see you're okay."

"I'm fine. Now can you let me go please?"

"Sorry." Lyssa quickly let go of Lana and sat down to her left.

Lyssa looked over at Julius and bit the bottom of her lip. She was not really good at apologies. Should she tell him she was sorry for blowing up at him yesterday? If she was honest with herself, she was definitely intrigued with these people, these so-called Guardians of the Watch Tower. Lyssa did want to know more about them, and already had that drive within her to make the world a better place. Vanquishing the evil she had always felt lurking in the darkness had always been her main goal. They were offering her an olive branch; and besides Jackson and Lana, what other ties did she have to the world? "Julius, I...well, I don't quite know what to say."

"Don't thank me. It was Hunter that convinced me that you would need proof of her safety before you could move forward with us."

"You okay then, Lana? Any shadows follow you home?"

"No shadows, but I did get a phone call from someone unexpected." She lifted her eyes to her knowingly and winked.

"Oh? Was it that new guy you've been eyeing in your political science class?" She would miss the guy surfing with Jackson and Lana. They'd sit on the quad and look out at the sea of men before them, picking the hotties from the not so hot, and the straight ones from the ones who were pretending to be straight, but were quite clearly closeted.

"Actually, it was someone I met at the bowling alley a few weeks ago."

"Wait, which one was that one? Is he as cute as the guy I met at Pride last year?" Jackson asked Lana inquisitively.

As it was clear that they were going to spend some time talking about their lives before the shadows entered them, the other men decided to leave them in peace. She could have sworn she heard Hunter's thoughts whisper: *Does this mean she is unattached*? Lyssa shook her head slightly and crinkled her eyes.

"What's wrong, Lyssa?" Lana asked her.

"Well," she started to say, but then lowered her voice to a whisper. "It's that guy, Hunter."

"You like him, don't you? Already daydreaming about the stud muffin?" Jackson rarely got the chance to tease her about these things, so it was no surprise he did not skip a beat. His head turned at an angle with a bright smile and teasing eyebrows.

"Shut it." The blush crept up her cheeks anyway, and the heat in her face made her feel like she had just eaten too much sugar.

"He seemed to stare extra hard at you, Lyssa."

Sadness overcast her face. "That's not funny, Jackson. If anyone ever understood me, it's you. I'm not his type."

"You're unlimited, Lyssa. In every way. You've never seen the beauty that others see. No matter what your shape or size, you are beautiful. And my god honey, you could eat butter off those curves. I'll never understand why people don't respect the power of a real woman." He snapped his fingers in the air and then said, "M'kay?"

Lyssa immediately burst into a giggling fit and covered her mouth quickly. "Have I told you lately how much I love you?" Jackson always knew what to say to her. He never let her feed her inner demons whenever he was around. He held her up when the only person who pushed her down was herself.

"You never have to. It's mutual, my dear."

"Oh my god, can we please stop with the love fest already?"

"Gagging are you?" Lyssa poked Lana on the arm and laughed.

"What do you think?" Lana shook her head while looking up at the ceiling.

"So, you really think we should do this?" Lyssa could not help but change the subject to the topic they all seemed to be ignoring.

"Yes, I do. You were always destined for something greater." The seriousness of Lana's tone was not lost on her.

"Greater than what? I never imagined my path could go in this direction. Hell, I don't even know what direction I'm going in. I mean, do you see any roads from here?"

Jackson turned his head over his shoulder, searching for any eyes that could be prying into their conversation, before turning back to her. "Look. The way I see it, we were unhappy down there with the direction our lives were moving. That was not going to change any time soon. Let's just see if this road takes us somewhere interesting. You were born to be fabulous, darling!"

"So were you!" Lyssa took a deep breath and really listened to what Jackson was saying. Never, not in her entire life, had Jackson ever told her something if he did not believe it.

"Well, I hate to cut this short, but I do have a class to get to. We're having a test in psychology today, and I can't afford to miss it."

"This is goodbye again, isn't it?" Lyssa let out a deep breath and shook her head.

"Not forever. You can still see me when you need me." Lana patted Lyssa's arm, but it was small consolation.

"How will we not need you?" She wanted to fight the grown up inside, for she did not want to be strong. Lyssa did not want to change, but the fight was short-lived. The adult persevered.

"You've survived far worse than this alone. You have people surrounding you here. Learn what you can, and then you can share it with my coven. I will always be here, Lyssa."

Jackson stood up and put his arms around both of the girls, then hummed a few lines and sang, "No matter how far apart we are."

Lyssa put a hand over his mouth and cut him off before he could belt out any words. Laughter left her mouth once more, for his antics always kept her amused. Lyssa smiled softly at him and lowered her hand. "I suppose that's a compromise I must make. I know you're right, Lana. I'm supposed to be here. It may not have happened the way it should have, but I do think I would have found my way here eventually. But seriously, did you look out the window?"

"Yea. Those stars underneath us are a little trippy. I'll be quite happy to return to the ground. Don't worry. You'll both visit soon. I'm sure of it."

"They'll have to chain me up to keep me away. Besides, I'll have to check out this new guy of yours."

"Speaking of guys, here comes yours." Jackson poked her in the side of the ribs.

"Shh!" Lyssa poked him back, glanced toward the door, and tried to shut her mind off. If only he would move a little faster and less like a panther prowling for his dinner. She could see the muscles under the shirt he was wearing today, and while she was not normally a muscle girl, his pecs were fantastic. Shaking her head, she cleared her thoughts, for she did not need anyone reading those.

"It's time." Hunter gestured to Lana, and she nodded at him. Lyssa knew she had to go this time, but this goodbye was easier.

Chapter 6

It didn't take long for Hunter to return. As soon as he did, he gestured for them to follow him and led them to the library. The walls were lined with books, from the bottom shelf all the way to the top. Various chairs were available to sit in, and a few lamps that lit the room brightly enough to read in any corner. A fireplace was set amidst more inlaid shelves, and its light flickered around them.

In the middle of the room sat a wide round table with a large sphere set into the center that rotated slowly. She could see the sphere spinning through an opening on the top of the table. When she expected to see the bottom of the sphere underneath the table, she was surprised to see the flat underbelly of the table. Lyssa should have known better than to expect things to be as they appeared. This was not an ordinary house.

"Sit, Lyssa. Jackson." Julius, who was already seated at the table, gestured to the chairs opposite him. Walking quietly over to the chairs, she tried hard to ignore all the eyes that were boring into her. Serena and Logan were already seated at the table. Jackson sat down in the chair to her right.

"Okay then." Lyssa looked at Julius and raised her nose higher in the air. It was her best effort to show she was being serious, to demonstrate that she was in fact ready to hear what he had to say, whereas before, she had only wanted to shut their entire world out. Looking at them each in turn, she took in the solemn faces. Even Serena had a calmness about her that she would not have suspected before.

They placed their arms on the table, and Lyssa could see that each one had a tattooed number four on their forearm. This must have meant something, but she had very little time to ponder this strange tattoo before they closed their eyes and a faint hum of energy started to swirl around them. The black ink on their arms changed, slowly at first. The ink appeared to be shifting out of their skin, and a white light was coming in to fill its space.

Lyssa had many questions, but they all seemed to still within her, for she sensed that now was not the time. As she closed her eyes, she took a deep breath. Then she let a calm rainbow of light run from the top of her head to the bottom of her toes, grounding her in its positive light. Lyssa felt it swarm around her, her gentle companion in her darkest hours. It streamed in front of her and added itself to the energy that was swirling around the group.

When she felt heat on her left forearm, she tried to push aside the nagging feeling that something was touching her. The energy around her changed as the warmth carved its way into her arm. She opened her eyes and tried not to panic as a number four started to appear on her arm. The ink was sliding into her skin, much like ink from a pen to paper, painlessly. Part of her wanted to rebel against this magic, but she knew it was inevitable, that this was par for the course. The biggest question she had right now was, why the number four?

"It's our sector number. We hold these things high: Life, Love, Peace, and Balance." Julius opened his eyes after he uttered those four words. "All guardians have always held these four beliefs among the highest. We treasure life. We do what we can to promote peace. We bring balance when chaos reigns."

"And we love those who often cannot see love for themselves." Hunter spoke without opening his eyes.

Lyssa almost shivered at Hunter's interruption. Something about him made her want to run. Jackson must have caught her discomfort, for his foot tapped hers lightly under the table.

"So that's it? Life, love, peace, balance? Four things. And we track down things that do not coexist with that philosophy. Sounds simple enough. Where do we start?" Lyssa tried to make her sarcasm ring out in a more appropriate tone. While her guide had told her to relinquish her past, it had formed her into the woman before them. If they expected her to suddenly morph into the perfect woman, they were mistaken. That would take some sparkling miracle, and Lyssa felt fresh out of those.

"Don't be too eager," Serena warned her. "You still have much to learn."

"But the shadows…," Lyssa started to say.

"Are always there." Julius looked at her seriously. "You have to train before we send you out. If you go off all half-cocked at the shadows, as you did yesterday, you could do serious harm to yourself and to others."

"Fine. What then?" Lyssa wanted to clash with him, to spark some kind of reaction from Julius that would distract from the lack of experience she had. Deflection, she was good at it. It had served her well her entire life, helping her deal with the firestorm around her. She had felt so powerful among her friends at college, safe and content with the path they were traveling together. They were young; they thought they could take on the world with no consequences at all. Lyssa had felt so sure of what she was doing then, and while that part of her life was just twelve hours ago, it seemed far away. Now, she felt as if she was at the low end of the totem pole, someplace she had never wanted to be again. Being a missing guardian had sounded so important, but clearly she was just a small piece of this collective puzzle.

"We start your training." Julius moved his hand over the globe in front of him, giving it a small push to make it spin faster. "Find them."

"Find who?" Did he want her to find the shadows? They could be anywhere right now, especially if they rose up from the ground. Was he kidding her?

"Find the shadows."

"Seriously? You want me to just look at this globe and tell you where the shadows are?" Lyssa started to laugh nervously, like it was some joke she was pretending to laugh at because she didn't quite understand the punch line.

"Show them, Lyssa," encouraged Jackson.

Lyssa looked over at him and nodded, then turned her gaze from his face. She reached out to touch the large globe that stretched across the table. Closing her eyes, she let her mind free itself from the moment. Lyssa ignored the sounds of each breath of air around her and felt herself letting go of any preconceptions she had made about this exercise as she let the moment take her. Electricity entered her body when her hand ran across a certain area on the globe. It felt threatening, but it was not the feeling she got from the shadows. "There is something here, but it does not feel like the shadows. What could it be?"

"Probably another source of corruption. Evil exists in many forms, Lyssa. Different sectors are more than likely dealing with them. At this point Sector 4 and several others are sanctioned to deal with the shadows."

"Alrighty then." While she felt her fingers pause on the spot once more, she knew she had to keep moving. Lyssa let more of the globe pass through her fingers before she felt something that made her stop the globe mid spin.

"Here." Lyssa pointed to the spot where she felt the darkness and opened her eyes. She was surprised to find that she had pointed to a place she was actually quite familiar with: St. Louis, Missouri. The energy pulsed from the dot on the globe to her fingertips.

"Well done. That has been one of the top ten places where we've detected them."

"So now what? Do we go after them?"

"You must start your training first."

"Fine. Where do we begin?" Training, ha. No worries. It would be a piece of cake. She could handle anything they threw at her. Bring it on.

"For now you return home." Julius extended a hand to each of them to teleport them home.

Elissa Daye

Chapter 7

When Jackson and Lyssa were returned to campus, they were surprised to learn that their circumstances had changed. The dorm rooms that they had been living in were no longer available to them, a precaution that had to be made for their own personal safety. All of their items had been magically moved into a new apartment that was completely furnished and paid for by the Watch Tower. Apparently, when magic was involved, the natural economy they had become accustomed to no longer existed. Room and board was no longer a hardship for either of them, which was completely unreal for both. It took a few moments for them to take it all in, but they adjusted well to the idea after a while.

Both of them were to continue as usual, assuming a dual identity to protect their roles at the Watch Tower. With their feet on the ground during the days, they were able to keep an eye out for activity around them while pursuing everyday lives. Lyssa was surprised how easy it was to get back into the swing of things; that when she was in the real world, her time at the Watch Tower had seemed almost non-existent. That was until she saw Hunter walking around campus. When she stopped in her tracks, Jackson was unprepared. His arm bumped into her, making her books drop from her hands, and she fell to her knees to pick them up.

"Here, let me help you." Hunter walked over to her and bent down to help her.

"I'm such a moron. Thank you. I really should pay more attention."

"It's not your fault, Lyssa. I believe I startled you." Hunter smiled softly at her.

"When did you start going here?" Jackson looked at Hunter skeptically.

"Down boy!" whispered Lyssa through clenched teeth.

"I've been around for a while, Jackson. I transferred in a few years ago to the veterinary program. I have another year before internship."

"I thought I'd seen you around here before. I've heard good things about that program. A friend of mine had her ferret's tumor biopsied and sent to the college's animal hospital." Lyssa would never forget the little ferret.

"What was its diagnosis?" Hunter looked at her with concern on his face. It was easy to see he was compassionate to animals.

"Not good, I'm afraid. Her Lily passed away last year. Poor thing, such a trooper too! Her lymph nodes had swollen up so much that she looked like she tried to swallow acorns."

"Was that Jaina's ferret?" Jackson interjected into the conversation, and his pointed stare brought Lyssa back to reality.

"Yes. Oh excuse me. We must be keeping you from your class." Lyssa nibbled on her bottom lip, suddenly conscious of the attention he was paying to her. It was so easy to talk to him, which was bizarre to her. She had always had trouble talking to men that she found attractive; it's what Jackson called her sabotage mechanism.

"Actually, I'm glad I ran into you. Julius wanted to start some specialized training with you tonight. He thought that perhaps a less magical approach to contacting you might be appropriate. I was going to call you later."

Lyssa wondered for a moment how he would have her phone number, but then reminded herself that the Watch Tower had provided that when they moved into their apartments as well. She was glad that question had not left her mouth, for she would have felt foolish. "What time?"

"Some time after dinner."

"Great. We're going to eat at the diner on Fifth Street, if you'd like to join us?" Jackson's proposal almost made Lyssa choke. He eyed her with a knowing look, and his nose turned up in merriment.

"I have to pass tonight, but rain check?" Hunter's eyes look apologetic.

"Sure. See you around." Lyssa pulled on Jackson's arm and they moved away from Hunter. When they were several steps away from him, Lyssa sighed. "You know that was code for 'I'm not interested.'"

Jackson turned around and looked back to where Hunter stood. "Oh honey, he's interested. By the way, he's looking at your behind; the boy is definitely into you."

"What?" Lyssa turned back to look at Hunter, but he had disappeared from sight. "That wasn't funny, Jackson!"

"Believe me or not. I call it the way I see it, Lyssa. I guess I'll buckle down and get some reading done tonight while you're gone. I have some books on astral projection and mythical creatures that I borrowed from the Watch Tower library."

"Sounds fascinating. I bet you wish you could get in on the action tonight."

"There will be other nights, Lyssa."

They continued on their way and separated when they made it to their classrooms. Lyssa nodded to Jackson one last time. "See you at dinner."

After dinner, Lyssa teleported to the Watch Tower and made her way into the library. Thankfully, Julius had taught her the spell before bringing her back to the campus. It was an easy spell to master and gave her more freedom. "Julius, Hunter said you wanted to do some training. I'm here...what did you have in mind?" Lyssa looked away from him uncomfortably, for his eyes seemed to pry into the deepest part of her.

"Wand at the ready." He was wearing black from his head to his toes, with the only contrast the silver pentacle he wore around his neck. He carried his wand in his hand and gestured for her to follow him.

"What?" Was he going to blast her with his wand? This man was seriously lacking communication skills.

"Have your wand at the ready. We are going in." He moved a book from the shelf and let it fall back in place. Apparently half of the bookshelf was a decoy, as that part of the wall swung inward to reveal a secret passage.

"Um, Julius. My wand broke when the shadows attacked, remember? How am I supposed to have my wand?" Wand at the ready? This guy was insane, just plain batty. Lyssa fought not to voice her concerns regarding his mental capacity as she scuffed the floor with a nervous slide of her foot.

"Ask and you shall receive." He waved his hand in the air, and several wands were suddenly floating in the air. "Pick one."

"Really? Alrighty then." Lyssa chose a wand made from elm with a perfectly shaped amethyst crystal on the end. When she picked it up, it felt as if it had been made for her. The instant it touched her fingers, the other wands disappeared. She could feel the hum of energy pulsing through the wood to her skin. This wand was really nothing short of spectacular.

"Ready then?"

"I guess." Lyssa really had no idea what she was supposed to be ready for at the moment...ready to follow him into a dark passage? Not really, but what choice did she have if she wanted to become one of them?

"Don't guess. Know." Julius let out a frustrated huff of air and looked back at her with one eyebrow raised.

"Fine! I'm ready." Her answer seemed to please him this time, as a small smile curled on his bearded face before he turned back around.

Lyssa followed him into the darkness and felt a blast of cold air on her face as she entered the tunnel. Holding up her wand, she asked it to light the way. It glowed eerily, breaking up the void in front of her.

It was not your typical hidden passageway. From what she could see, it went from the wooden walls of the house and turned into a smaller tunnel that was formed into the dirt. She knew instantly that she should keep her guard up. The house itself was not connected to the ground, so as to keep it free from the grasp of the shadows, so how was there dirt in a passageway?

After a few feet, there was a larger opening. She walked behind Julius, trusting that he would not lead her into something she could not handle. Lyssa assumed that this was a magical place he had created to help her practice finding the shadows.

When she exited the tunnel, she found herself at the end of a long alley; the tunnel she had just left closed up behind her. There were dumpsters scattered along the alley that smelled of rotting food, and cardboard boxes were slanted against dark brick walls. It looked like an alley one might find in any big city, with tall buildings lined with apartments and fire escapes. When Lyssa looked up, she could see many windows with their lights turned off, so the only illumination came from the glare reflected off the glass panes from the light poles outside. A handful of windows had a faint glow through the curtains, most likely lit from televisions inside. There were a couple of doors leading inside to small businesses on her left that lay quiet in their nightly slumber. Wherever they were, it was late, and it was clear that most of this world was already asleep.

Julius stopped at the end of the tunnel and motioned for her to step closer. "I'll be right behind you, Lyssa. I want to see what you can do."

"Great." Fan-freaking-tastic! If he could see her feet sticking to the ground, he would know that she was not quite looking forward to leaping out of the dark alley to find a shadow to attack. Steeling her nerves, she reminded herself that it was just a test, and that nothing could hurt her. She took a deep calming breath and moved in front of him. "Here goes nothing."

Lyssa scanned her environment, searching for any movement that would indicate a shadow was near. She did not have to wait long. The sound of a crying woman could be heard a few streets away. The cry itself was not unworldly...it was the way the hair on her neck rose in response. A shadow must be lurking close to her. It had probably been following that poor woman for some time. She looked back at Julius and motioned for him to follow her.

Walking about half a block, Lyssa turned to the left, to where she had heard the woman's cries. On the ground near a window she saw it, like the black smoke of a burning tire, moving so slowly she had to really squint to see it better. Like the others, it was shaped like a human, and was peering into a window with glowing yellow eyes.

"You there," she yelled at it. "Step away from that window!" Lyssa pointed her lit wand at it menacingly, and heard a low growl as it turned her way. If it had a mouth, she imagined it would be sneering at her right now. Its eyes turned from a bright yellow to an eerie orange, as if to tell her that it had not liked her intruding upon its nightly hunt. It moved faster than she expected for something that floated so soundlessly across the ground. Its bottom never touched the sidewalk, yet she knew it drew its strength from the land beneath it.

"I warned you!" Sending all her energy into the wand in her hand, she conjured a blast of light that sent the shadow reeling. Lyssa continued to shoot blast after blast at it until it dissipated completely before her. When she sensed the arrival of more shadows from the street behind them, she turned to meet the challenge.

"Bring it!" Lyssa clenched her teeth together and glared at the shadows in front of her. When they started to get closer, she drew two lines in the air with her wand and watched them try to cross it. When the first one got too close to the first line, the light wrapped itself around the shadow and tightened around it like a lasso. The second one backed up and reassessed its attack. She sent the line of light after it, and it chased the shadow down the road.

"Faster!" she ordered it. The light sped through the air so fast that the shadow had no time to act. Soon, it was wrangled up like the first one. "Any use for these two, Julius?"

"None." He looked at her with a smirk as she made the conjured lassos pull the shadows so tightly that they exploded into dust before them.

"Well?" She looked over at Julius to see if she had succeeded with her challenge for the night.

"That's enough for tonight." He grabbed onto her arm and waved his wand quickly before him.

Here we go again, she thought to herself. She would have been just as happy walking back into the tunnel to the house. It also annoyed her that if they were going to teleport, he had not allowed for her to go by herself. She was quite capable. At least they were back inside the library before she knew it.

"How'd I do? That was quite a course, Julius. Everything felt so real. It felt like I was really there."

"You were." He chuckled, as if laughing at a private joke.

"What?" Was he saying that those were real shadows?

"Yes, Lyssa. Those were real shadow people."

Lyssa sat down at the table with the inlaid globe that was now still. A small dot of light had appeared where the city of St. Louis was supposed to be. "Did you take me to St. Louis?" She really did not need him to respond, for she knew the answer before she had opened her mouth. She sighed deeply. "You realize that keeping things from me will not get you very far. I want some answers now! For starters, where the hell are we?"

"What do you mean?" He was obviously dodging her questions yet again.

"This house, Julius. Where is it? Are we in space?"

"This is the Watch Tower. It exists everywhere and nowhere."

"So, that's a 'no' to outer space, then? That's a relief. I was afraid if I walked out the door that I might be sucked into some kind of airless vacuum. I guess that means it's safe to go outside."

"That's not quite accurate. Just follow protocol, and you'll be fine." Julius waved her concerns off too easily.

The Land of the Shadows

"You really are ill-prepared for me, aren't you? Yet, you've known about me for how long? How did you know there was another guardian? How did you know it was me?"

"We've been waiting a long time for you, Lyssa. However, you were off our radar for quite a while. It wasn't until you started attacking the shadows that we were able to locate you. I've never had to train someone from the ground up, Lyssa. You have a lot of true talent. You just need to hone it while you learn to use the rest of your skills."

"How many more are there, Julius?"

"I wondered when you would get around to that. There are more scattered across different places in this world." He sat down at the table and pushed a button that was near his chair, which made a screen come out of the ceiling. He gestured to the screen, and she kept her eyes on it.

"If you see here, these lights are the Guardians of the Watch Tower."

White flashing lights appeared all over the map on the screen. There were a lot more lights than she thought there would be. It was good to know that so many people were watching over their world, but that did not explain everything to her. "You say this house is the Watch Tower. It can't possibly contain all the guardians."

"You have much to learn, Lyssa. There are places in this house you've still not seen. It is much larger than you know. There are rooms upon rooms, which are accessible when you are ready. You will have plenty of time to meet more guardians, but for now, you will become more familiar with this sector: Sector 4. In time, you will meet others. Don't wish for too much at once. It will make your head spin."

"Thank you for answering my questions, Julius." While he still had not shared much with her, she was happy for the little information that he had finally given. She still could not believe he had taken her into a dangerous situation without telling her first. That proved one of two things. Either he trusted her abilities enough to give her a chance, or he really had no clue what he was doing. Maybe it was a mixture of the two.

"We are done for the moment. Food will be served in a little while if you want to stick around."

Chapter 8

When Lyssa returned to their apartment, Jackson was already in bed. At breakfast, he had already left for class. She did not see him until she returned later that afternoon. Jackson was watching TV in the living room. "How was training?"

"It went well. I did not expect it to be so real. I thought Julius would let me get my feet wet with some practice dummies, or something like that. I didn't expect him to throw me right into it." It was true, Julius had literally thrown her to the wolves, but somehow she knew that he had a reason for it. The shadows they faced were numerous, and they grew far and wide each day. Soon, the world would be crawling with them, blocking the dots of light she had seen on the map. She wondered how many guardians they lost each year to their causes. She understood that Julius could not wait for her to do the years of training that they must have had.

"He shouldn't rush things."

"He does seem to have a leadership problem."

"As in how the hell did he ever become leader?" Jackson shook his head in disgust.

"Exactly, but maybe he was chosen the way we were."

"It's possible."

"What do you have planned for the rest of the week, Jackson?"

"Just spending some time relaxing in between tests…and you?"

"The same. I'm going to go study at the library. See you later."

They each spent the next few weeks getting back into their daily schedule, while also adding in their new responsibilities. Hunter had become an easy fixture in their lives too. Lyssa could not believe that she had missed his face on campus before. She may have seen him around a few times, but it was certainly easier to notice him now.

Today, Lyssa planned to check out a new store in the area. For some reason she was drawn to it. She turned to Jackson, who was studying at the kitchen table next to her. "A new thrift store just opened. I wanted to check it out. Do you want to come with me?"

"I suppose it would be better than sitting around here."

"Hey, you could still be stuck in the dorm. At least our apartment doesn't smell like stinky armpits."

Jackson crinkled his nose. "Well that is certainly one upgrade we can thank the Watch Tower for. Rent free apartment living away from campus."

"It's nice not to have to worry about these things. The scholarships to our school help too. With all this magic and know how, we'll be set for life."

The doorbell rang, and Jackson walked over to answer it. When he peered in the eyehole, he turned back to Lyssa. "It's your lover boy."

"What?" Lyssa rushed over to the door and gasped. What was Hunter doing there? Not that she minded. They had all been spending more time together on campus lately, but he had never come to their apartment before. Hunter was a decent human being, something she had not quite expected for someone so beautiful. She hated to be judgmental, because she certainly knew how it felt to be judged. The years of bullying, the pressures of being different from everyone else around her, were never buried deep enough in her consciousness.

A flash entered her mind with the image of a girl who stood on the wall unnoticed, while all the pretty people walked past her with their perfect worlds intact. Lyssa was the girl who stayed still and quiet, holding her breath, hoping that people passing would not have a chance to see the old hand-me down clothes and the ill-fitting shoes. It was hard to have a target painted on her head when it always seemed to be deer season. High school had been a disaster waiting to happen for her. It had been bad enough to have had to deal with all of this at school, but then she had to return home, to a place where things happened to her that had been so much more threatening than these shadow people ever could be.

It was true that Lyssa had spent a lifetime dodging the labels that other people had put on her, so she did feel guilt when she compared Hunter to a fancy bauble. He was just so shiny, but she reminded herself that he was unexpectedly nice to her, and that sometimes you had to look past what you saw to understand the person beneath. Hunter genuinely seemed to care about her well-being and making sure that she adjusted well to her dual-life as an everyday college student and a Guardian of the Watch Tower. It actually made him all the more attractive to her.

"Are you two going to answer the door or not?" Clearly, he was amused.

"Sorry. One moment." Lyssa unbolted the door and opened it. "Come in."

"Welcome to our humble abode," offered Jackson. He swept his arm over his stomach as he bowed before him.

"I see you got the standard issue apartment too." A big grin filled his face.

"Yep. Boring. I'm going to paint the walls deep purple and blue here soon."

"You could requisition for that…unless you know the spell for it." Hunter gestured to the walls.

"I'm afraid we're a little short stacked on glamour spells at the moment. I'm sure Jackson can find the right spell in one of his books though. What brings you here, Hunter? Not that you're not welcome, of course."

"To be honest, I was bored. I needed some fresh air and a friendly face or two." If he caught her uneasiness, he didn't let on.

"Lyssa was just about to head out to the new thrift store. I bet she would love some company."

Traitor. Lyssa narrowed her eyes on Jackson and felt her big toe curl in her shoe, the one safe gesture of shyness she had; as long as her shoes were on, it was not a sign of weakness, for no one could see it. "Uh, yeah. You're welcome to come with me if you like."

"The new one on Center Street?"

"I believe that's the one, yes. Did you want to go?" Lyssa fidgeted with her fingers for a moment, then forced herself to put them behind her back. Why did it feel like she was asking him out on a date? They were simply going on a walk.

"Sure."

"Are you coming, Jackson?" Lyssa grabbed her purse and jacket.

"Sorry. Have things to do. Have fun kiddos." Jackson almost bolted from the room, and Lyssa wanted desperately to call him back. She was usually more confident around people, but Hunter made her nervous, and while he was a handsome man, she knew there was something else to it, something she had not quite been able to put her finger on yet.

"Shall we?"

"After you." Lyssa followed Hunter out the door.

It was a short walk to the thrift store, which was spent in an unusually peaceful silence. Lyssa was thankful for the silence, for the way her heart beat rapidly in her chest, she was sure to make a fool of herself if she opened her mouth. Hunter made her whole body flutter whenever he was around her, and she was not quite sure how to handle it. He was not the typical man she was interested in...not that she had a type per se, but it typically was someone less noticeable to the female population, the trustworthy type who, while still attractive, would be safe enough for her not to fall completely in love with. Falling for the wrong man could be devastating, and she refused to do it.

When they made it to the thrift store, Hunter opened the door and held it for her to enter. "Ladies first."

Her cheeks flushed hot against the cool burst of air escaping through the doorway. "Thank you."

"I'm going to check out the books." Hunter gestured to the wall. "I like to find vintage classics."

"Go right ahead. I'm going to look over here first." Lyssa found her way over to the glass case on the other side of the room. She peered inside and was eyeing a necklace when the saleslady came over. She had a small gold locket in her hand that she was about to put inside the case.

"Can I see that?" Something about the locket caught her eye, and Lyssa had to figure out why.

"Of course!" The tiny brunette handed over the locket and smiled at her.

The heart-shaped locket was old and worn. Two faces were peering back at her when she opened the clasp. Small flashes of light entered her mind, images from another life. A man and a woman deeply in love, a romance that had seemed timeless that had ended tragically. Pain filled her very soul until small droplets pooled at the corners of her eyes. Lyssa blinked them away and shook her head.

Lyssa looked inside the locket again and touched the faded photos inside it. The two faces were older, but the woman looked very similar to what Lyssa looked like in this lifetime. Perhaps the nose or ear was off just a little, but it was eerily close. And the man was familiar too…Hunter. Almost every part of his face was the same, except for the dimple in the middle of his chin. Lyssa now understood why his presence had seemed so second nature to her. Lyssa believed in past lives and had actually recovered several of them through past life regression therapy with Lana.

"Lyssa? Are you okay?" Hunter put a hand on her shoulder.

She closed her eyes and shook her head to chase away the memories tied into the necklace in her hand. Closing the locket quickly, she closed her fingers around it. "Sorry. That was weird."

Hunter's eyes touched on the locket in her hand. "Can I see that?"

It was a demand that Lyssa was not prepared to follow. "Why?"

"Just give it here, Lyssa." Hunter looked inside, and the same familiar glow filled his eyes. He closed the locket and looked at Lyssa.

His blue eyes met hers, and in that moment they both seemed to know what the universe was telling them. They had known each other many lifetimes ago. Hunter grabbed her hand and walked her over to the counter. "We'll take this."

"I can get it," Lyssa interrupted him. She yanked it from his hands and put it on the counter to check out. Her chin jutted out defiantly against the protest that never came. When she had finished paying, they walked out of the store in an uneasy silence.

"We need to go somewhere to talk."

"About?" Lyssa refused to look at him.

"A lot of things." Hunter reached for her hand, and his eyes pleaded for her to grab onto him. Lyssa gave an exasperated sigh and grabbed onto his hand. Within moments, they were speeding through the air.

Elissa Daye

Chapter 9

When they finished their journey, Lyssa found they were sitting in a small garden at a place she did not recognize. While she had never been there before, it felt safe. She let go of his hand and put a few steps between them.

"Come here." He reached over and tried to take her hand again. She tried desperately to retract it, but he was quicker than her. His fingers splayed over hers, and she felt the warm comfortable feeling start to rush back into her, the same feeling she'd felt when she picked up the locket. There was something in the energy he sent that created a sad echo between them, like a trace of a long lost loved one who had suddenly returned. She looked up at his face in confusion; the emotions that raced through her left her perplexed.

Hunter raised his hand up and brought it to her face, but she could not stand the closeness any longer. "What are you doing?" Lyssa pushed away from him. "I don't like to be touched. Please don't."

"You've been hurt."

"I'm not hurt, I'm broken." She crossed her arms around her and turned her back to him. What was he doing? Why did he have to be so close to her? Being in this moment with him right now, with his eyes piercing her to the core, it was almost more than she could handle. Lyssa could not tell if he was coming on to her or if he pitied her.

Lyssa could hear him swear softly. She did not turn to see him walk closer to her; instead, she tried to shut out the sound of the blood pumping loudly in her ears. Closing her eyes, she grappled with the ugliness that she had locked away, but she knew it was useless. The memories were going to hit her again; a dark arm reaching across, trying to break her. A muffled cry that she had tried so many times to keep inside her mouth every time he entered the room was stuffed in the back of her throat like an old mothball. She shook her head with her eyes still closed, and almost jumped when she felt Hunter's hand on her shoulder.

"Lyssa." It was a soft caress across a stormy sea. It reached out like a lifeline, and her soul latched onto it hungrily. Hunter tried to pull her into his arms, and she ached to go into them willingly. As much as she wanted to appear stiff and unyielding, she longed to bend. When was the last time she had let someone comfort her? When was the last time she had let it out? When would she be able to let go of the past?

Lyssa turned to face Hunter and looked up into his eyes. They were smoky and sensuous while soft and comforting at the same time. If this was a test, she had the distinct suspicion that she was failing miserably. "Hunter." Lyssa walked into his arms and rested her head on his shoulder.

"I've missed you." He ran his arm up and down her back to soothe the memories away.

Did he just say he'd missed her? How do you miss someone you never really knew? "What did you say?" She pushed gently away from his body and looked at him with quiet concern.

"Lyssa, there is so much you won't understand yet, so much that perhaps you never will." Sadness crossed over his face.

He was so close to her, she could almost feel his breath on her face."What do you need me to understand?"

"That every life is filled with second chances."

Lyssa knew he was referring to what she had seen when she picked up the locket. "Karma, the wheel of life? Perhaps there was a reason it did not end well the first time?" Lyssa shrugged off the part of her that wanted to cling to the idea that destiny could very well be throwing them back together. She did not know him well enough to have those thoughts yet.

"We just didn't have the right circumstances before. I've known you from the moment I saw you. I felt it. Didn't you?"

"Well, to be honest, I had a lot of other things on my mind at the time. You'll have to forgive me if some psychic bond to the afterlife never formed in my head. But I must ask, if you knew the moment you saw me, why didn't you say anything? And hypothetically speaking, why is it that only you remembered everything?"

"I wish I could say for sure. I think we all carry different things with us. I didn't have the same burdens to carry in this life, not like you did. Maybe now you will remember more." He ran a finger through the curl trying to escape her hair tie.

It was nice to think that they had some connection that brought them together, but a sad thought entered her mind. "What if I don't remember it all, Hunter?"

"Then we begin again, Lyssa. I know you have some feelings for me. No matter how hard you try, you can't shut them off. I feel them here." He put his hand over her heart, and she took a deep breath.

He was right. She did feel something for him, and it did feel like more than just some kind of attraction. "But you don't really know me, Hunter. What if I am nothing like the person I was?" Was she enough? How could she measure up to a memory of someone she used to be, if she had no idea who that was supposed to be?

"I look in your eyes, Lyssa, and I know everything that matters." He smiled at her in such a way that if he asked her to walk out the door with him right now she'd go, no matter the destination. "It's true. We haven't known each other long in this lifetime, Lyssa. But my soul will always remember."

Lyssa's heart started to turn over in her chest, and a slight flitter of hope ran through her. Maybe it was time to trust someone for a change, to find happiness in a moment, even if the future wasn't a promise. "Where do we go from here, Hunter?"

Hunter pulled her closer to him. His face fell closer to hers, and she had the distinct impression that he was going to kiss her. Lyssa felt a need to flee, but her feet remained planted firmly on the ground, and her arms were suddenly lacking any motivation to push him away. She felt his breath close to her lips, and the last chance to move ended.

His lips hit hers before she could mutter a protest, and the warmth seeping from them was unexpected. Raising her hands to his chest, she grabbed a fistful of his shirt. Fighting an internal battle no one watching would see, flashing images entered her head so quickly she almost felt dizzy. His hand brushed across her face, and she could hear the small exhale of air when he moved his face away from hers. She pulled closer to him and put her head on his shoulder, allowing her to avoid his probing eyes. There was something unusual about this moment in time, as the heartbeat at his throat pounded deliciously in her ears. It was new, but somehow it felt old and comfortable at the same time…as if this had happened to her before.

"Okay. That's enough for now." Hunter stepped away from her.

"Wait." Her voice was soft and shaky when it left her mouth. "Why?"

He did not turn around, and she so desperately wanted to see his face. Was he laughing at her? Was this funny to him? What exactly was this supposed to be? When he did finally turn around, his features were schooled perfectly. "Because I remember." Hunter let the words hang in the air.

"I wish I could." The words left her mouth in a desperate whisper.

He turned to face her and smile softly at her, the sadness replaced with hope. "One day at a time?" Hunter reached out his hand to her.

"Yes. I think that would be best." Lyssa grabbed onto his hand and braced herself before they teleported back to her apartment.

Later that afternoon, Lyssa sat down at the table with the globe at the Watch Tower and let out a deep sigh. She was extremely confused about what had happened. When Lyssa tried to pull the flashing pictures back to the forefront of her mind, they just would not stick. It was hard at first, but when she put her mental feelers out there, she could sense the deep hurt Hunter was hiding as he left the garden, even though it would never show outwardly. It was a relief to see that the kiss had affected him as much as it had her, that a man could be sensitive to emotions.

It was her first real kiss, the only one that had made her tingle from her head to her toes. It's not like she had never dated anyone before or had a relationship. She'd certainly been kissed before, but it had never felt like that one. Everything dulled in comparison. If only she knew what he wanted from her.

Lyssa closed her eyes and tried to quiet the emotions raging through her. The stillness that usually came easily to her was non-existent, for his heart still beat loudly in her memory, and the warmth of his breath still lingered on her lips. It had only been a moment in time, but she was already haunted by it.

If Lyssa was honest with herself, she knew she had wanted him to kiss her. She'd wanted it from the first moment she saw him. It was scary to desire something so close, so easily within your reach, something you never dared imagine before. He was absolutely beautiful, and those eyes could easily put her in a trance. Should she let go and enjoy whatever moments she could have, or hold out so that she did not get her heart broken in the process? How could she trust someone when those she was supposed to trust in the past had left her torn to pieces? Perhaps it was time to listen to Jephilia and just let her past go.

Lyssa looked at the number four on her arm and traced it with her fingertip. Life, Love, Balance, Peace. She did not feel closer to understanding any of those things right now. If she were to be someone else, someone better, then she needed to work on these things.

Chapter 10

Later that same night, Hunter had returned to the Watch Tower. They both sat in the library in an uneasy silence as he read from his book and she stared at the spinning globe. When she was about to say something to him, he stood up and walked out of the room. She felt the loss of his energy the moment he left.

The room was empty without him, and Lyssa soon found herself following him. When she found him perched on a sofa in the upstairs sitting room, she knew what she had to do. His eyes were closed, and he was deeply concentrating on his meditation when she sat down next to him. She really did not know what to expect, but she took a chance and reached to put her hand over his and closed her eyes. When he made to move his hand, she held it down. "Please, Hunter. Stay. Please." Lyssa could not help the sound of sad desperation in her voice. She was fighting a battle that was hidden to herself. Lyssa had no idea that tears were falling down her face until Hunter raised his other hand to wipe them away. He pulled her into a warm embrace and she stayed there, feeling the rise and fall of his chest. She was at peace. There were no expectations, no unwieldy judgments, just silence. She had never been courageous enough to ask for what she needed, but Hunter did not need her to ask him for anything. It was as if he did know her, even better than she knew herself.

When the tears had passed, she moved back to sitting next to him and closed her eyes. She pulled her feet underneath her, and they sat quietly together, meditating in the peace that moved between them. This peace was not as alien to her as she thought it would be. An older part of her was buried deep under the walls that had been built in this lifetime. Lyssa could feel it now, just an inkling that she was not limited to how the world had raised her here. There was more: more to her, more to life, more to this world, and so much more to this universe than she imagined before.

How could she move on and be free from the darkness that clouded her youth? Lyssa suddenly knew the key. It was something she had been dreading, something she felt would one day need to be done, but she had never been ready to do. She had to put her pain to rest. It did not have to define her any longer. It did not have to drive everything she did. She would not be able to experience Life, Love, Balance, or Peace until she did something drastic. Her only choice was to do something dramatic, something so life changing, that up until now, she had feared it. She took a deep breath.

In the forefront of her mind the words rang out. They whispered inside her like a chanting reprieve that let go of the pain of her past.

I forgive you. I will no longer hold hate in my heart for the crimes you've committed against me. I let it go. From today on, you will touch my mind no longer. Rest in peace, Father.

Lyssa imagined the last time she had seen him. He had looked defeated, as if he had known she would never return for him to control again. She had never gotten to confront him for the evil he'd brought into her life, but she no longer needed to. None of that mattered anymore. She could feel the darkness that he had created as it slowly faded away. There was a stillness in her that no one else could have provided for her. She was free, and while she had thought it would take more than a lifetime to accomplish, or that it would never happen, the powers that those three words had set into motion were incredible. Free. At last.

Hunter touched her arm, and she looked over at him. "Lyssa, you're floating."

"What?" She had no idea what he was talking about.

"Look." He pointed at the couch.

Lyssa looked down and almost shrieked. He was right. She was floating inches above the couch. How in the world was she doing that? "Make it stop!" she said as she tried to fight the nervous giggles that were trying to escape her chest.

"No can do. You did it. You'll have to bring yourself down." His teasing smile calmed the nervousness she was feeling.

"Fine." Lyssa screwed her eyes shut so she would not see his teasing stares as she took a deep breath. If she made herself rise off the couch, she should be able to make herself stop floating. It took a few seconds for her to focus on her goal before she felt her bottom calmly touch the cushions once again. She opened her eyes and looked at Hunter.

"Feel better?"

"Actually, yes. I feel a lot better." Lyssa raised her hand up to his chin and smiled at him. She stood up and acted as if she were going to walk away. What happened next surprised both of them. Turning around, she leaned over and lowered her lips to his. Lyssa almost expected him to pull away, but when he pulled her closer, her heart started racing. She saw more images in her head. Two people, so deeply in love they did not notice the world around them. She could feel the laughter, the tears, and the love they shared. It happened in a dizzy whirl, and when she broke the kiss and looked at Hunter, she knew that he had felt it too.

"I will remember too, Hunter. I just need time and patience."

"And practice." Hunter pulled her back down for a kiss that stole the breath from her body and sent chills of anticipation down her spine, the kind of feeling that could make you forget where you were, which was clear when Logan's cough interrupted them. He flipped his brown hair out of his eyes and smiled at Lyssa.

Hunter's eyes shot daggers at Logan for his interruption. "Logan, don't you have something else to do right now?"

"Well, actually, no. Julius sent me to get Lyssa for training. If you want to explain to him why she isn't available right now, feel free." Logan smirked at Hunter. Clearly, he was not surprised to find them together.

"Training?" She looked apologetically at Hunter. "I should go. I'll see you later?"

"Count on it."

If she could bottle up the feelings his kiss sent through her and manufacture them for all the women of the world, she would be a rich woman. She still did not quite understand how this had started between them, but from this point on, she was not going to second-guess it. There was a strong connection between the two of them, and she would definitely be exploring the possibilities.

Another knock sounded, and it was not a surprise to see Serena trying to poke through the door. "Lunch is finished. I thought you might be hungry."

"We'll be down in a few minutes," Hunter told her quickly.

"Should I time you?" It was clear that the redhead was teasing them, for she did not wait for a response.

"Well, I guess we should go." Lyssa started to turn to the door, but Hunter put his hand on her arm and turned her back.

"Wait."

She was afraid to look up for a moment, for she did not trust herself to look at him calmly. Her heart was already pounding in her chest. Every second alone with him seemed slightly more dangerous than the seconds before. If she fell too deeply for him, she could be seriously hurt, but she had to find the courage, because she knew he would not give up. Lyssa looked up at him and saw that he smiled a soft challenge at her.

"No, I won't."

"Stop reading my mind," she tried to say, but the last word was cut off by the swift sweep of his lips across hers. She could not help the soft murmurs that left her mouth when his lips met hers. Kissing him forever would be easy, and she would not miss the air that she breathed. This kiss lasted longer than the others, and one led to several slower ones that made her skin flush from her throat all the way up to the top of her head. Lyssa had to push him away or they would never leave. They were both taking deep breaths after they disengaged.

"If you would just feel more and think less, I would have fewer thoughts to read." His joking smile put her back to a relaxed frame of mind, and she grabbed his hand, pulling him to the door.

"Let's go eat." They walked down the stairs, then down the hallway on the first floor to the dining room. The other guardians were already seated at the table, surrounded by plenty of food for everyone. She half wondered if the food had been cooked or conjured, as there were plenty of magical skills in this bunch. It was hard to believe things were happening the way they were. While Lyssa had an open mind when she started studying magic in college, she had no idea that the magical world extended much further than she had ever imagined. It was easy to believe in the possibility that there was magical energy around them everywhere. Lyssa had even felt some of its presence in her circles, but she had never felt so much within herself before now. She had no idea that she could actually bring so much energy forward from her wand, but had simply acted on impulse and made an assumption that it would be there to back her up. It made her wonder what she could have accomplished with her life before now if she had simply known all that she held inside her.

"I heard you knocked out some shadows the other day, Lyssa," Serena said with a voice that attempted polite chitchat.

Lyssa wondered if seeing her walking into the room with Hunter had made Serena realize that she was not after her precious Julius. They had still been holding hands when they walked in the door. It amazed her that Hunter had not made any effort to conceal their involvement. With their eyes on her, she could feel the scarlet that tried to mark her skin, but she fought the red inching up her neck. "Apparently." Lyssa looked over at Julius and wrinkled her nose.

Julius grinned mischievously. "We all have to start somewhere. You're a natural, Lyssa."

Wow. Did he just compliment her? Why was he in a good mood? Julius was sure hard to figure out. Perhaps someday she would understand what made him tick. "Thank you, Julius. At least you have become more detailed in your instructions, instead of winging it." She smirked at him and waited for the temper to rise back in his eyes, but it did not. Instead, he looked almost apologetic.

"You're right, Lyssa. That was tactless earlier. I should have told you it was not just a test."

Hunter was glaring at Julius, and it was clear that the apology that Julius spoke came from a steaming argument unspoken between them. "You got that right."

"Okay, look, if you are going to be mind speaking about the poor girl, perhaps I should teach her how to chime in?" Serena shook her head at the two of them. Her red hair was pulled out of her face today, and she looked younger than she had the first time Lyssa had seen her.

"I would appreciate that. I'm usually quite adept at reading minds, but the mind blocks you've all seemed to master are hard to get past." She smiled at Serena. Was it possible that Serena was more friend than foe now? Lyssa had the distinct impression when she first met her that Serena had wanted to scratch her eyes out. She was glad the feeling had passed.

"Perhaps later."

The rest of lunch went very quickly. There was so much she wanted to ask everyone, so many things that they had the advantage of already knowing. The problem was she had no idea where to start. Now she knew that this house was not in space, just in an intangible place where the shadows or any other magical being could not reach them. There were many other Guardians of the Watch Tower, and the Watch Tower itself was vaster than she could ever imagine. Lyssa wondered if the other wings of the Watch Tower were as old as this one. Not that she could complain.

"Serena?"

"Yes, Lyssa?"

"Can we work on keeping people out of my own thoughts first? I should be allowed some privacy, don't you think?" She looked pointedly over at Hunter. He could read her easier than everyone else, and it irked her to no end. No matter how handsome he was, he should understand simple boundaries. She stuck her tongue out at him when no one else was looking and chuckled when he almost choked on his drink.

"Yes. A girl does have to have her secrets. That will be the first thing I teach you."

Chapter 11

Lyssa was still fuming as she sat in the library of the Watch Tower. She had spent her morning in a heated battle with the Education Department at her college. Apparently, her lack of focus in her clinical observation class had given them some cause for concern. Lyssa had been called into their office and verbally berated for half an hour before she finally had it. When the bloated woman before her had asked her if she was sure she wanted to be a teacher, Lyssa did the only thing she could think of. She gave her a resounding no and told her that if being a teacher turned her into someone that made a living out of making others feel like crap, then she didn't want anything to do with it. She might have also told the head of the department something about Lyssa's tax dollars paying her salary, and that Lyssa wondered how many other perspective teachers they had bullied. After her encounter, she had gone directly to the guidance counselor and changed her major to a general Bachelor of Education, which would allow her to graduate a semester early if she finished the rest of her core requirements.

Lyssa was so wrapped up in her thoughts that she did not notice Serena and Jackson entering the room. When she finally looked up, she found both of them eyeing her speculatively. "What?" she snapped.

"Oh dear, rough day?" Jackson looked at her with concern.

"Well it started off well, but went downhill quickly. Let's just say I did something I had been debating over for quite some time."

"Well that sounds cryptic. Would you like to explain?" Serena walked over to the chair beside her and sat down.

"I told the head of my department to stuff it, pretty much. I quit my major before they could kick me out of it, and…well that's pretty much that." Lyssa took a deep breath and calmed herself. While she would like to say she was completely fine with her choice today, it was not the case. A very large part of her did not like to be told what she could or could not do, and she did not like her choices questioned. When they had asked her if she was sure she wanted to be a teacher, it was like her entire lifetime had flashed before her eyes. She had not been raised to believe in herself or to have any sense of pride in who she was, and she had fought hard to find an ounce of confidence. It seemed like she had to try much harder than most people to broadcast a strong woman to the world. Lyssa was anything but strong really, for the truth of it was that she had many insecurities that she battled every day.

"It was probably for the best, hon. Are you okay?" Jackson understood so much more than anyone else ever would be able to. He had lived under similar oppressive circumstances. While he made being absolutely fabulous seem easy, Lyssa understood the depth of emotions that lay beneath the surface. It was why every hair was always in place, and every wrinkle ironed out of his clothes before he left for the day. Ever partners in commiseration, the two of them would always be cemented in each other's lives.

"I'm fine." Fine, an emotional code they had conspired to create years ago…Fed up, Insecure, Neurotic, and Emotional. Today she felt like all them mixed into one.

They all turned when Hunter walked into the room. Lyssa's eyes met his and they each paused for a moment. She turned away first, uncomfortable with the probing message trapped within his gaze. "Everything all right?"

"We're just talking about going shopping," Serena offered up.

"Ah, I see. Well, have fun. Maybe I'll see you later?" Hunter asked them all politely.

"Well, I have a test to study for, and Serena, didn't you say we also had some training tonight?" Jackson initiated. While Julius had been mentoring Lyssa, Serena was in charge of Jackson's training.

"Oh, yeah. Lots of training, but Lyssa is free."

Lyssa did not miss the smirk that Serena sent her way. "I suppose. If I don't need to do training tonight—"

"Nope, she's free." Serena cut her off.

"Great. I'll see you later then, Lyssa." Hunter turned, gave her a half smile, and left the room.

"Alrighty then." Lyssa shook her head. Could they have been any more obvious that they were trying to push the two of them together? It wasn't a secret that Hunter and Lyssa might have a thing going on right now, but it wasn't exactly public either.

Serena smiled at her perceptively. "You're afraid of him, aren't you?"

"What? Why would I be afraid of him? He's been nothing but kind to me." Lyssa looked away uncomfortably.

"Well, it doesn't take an Einstein to see you've been hurt before, Lyssa. Nor is it hard to tell that you have some confused feelings about him."

Lyssa sighed deeply. "You're right, Serena. I'm every bit afraid of him. I'm just, well—"

"Afraid you might lose yourself?" Jackson interjected.

Damn it. He knew her too well. "If you say so, Jackson."

"I understand that more than you know. Things did not used to be the way they are now between me and Julius, but that is an entirely different story. We never had the history that you and Hunter do. For you, it is scary to crave someone more than air. You would do almost anything to hang on to it, even if you lost yourself in the process. You don't have to lose anything, Lyssa. Love shapes you into something deeper than you could ever imagine, and it makes you do things you never dreamed you could do."

"I never said anything about love, Serena. I don't know what I mean any more."

Serena giggled at her last statement. "Oh darling, you're going to be in much deeper than you thought before you know it."

"Is that a bad thing?"

"Heavens, no. Live. Love. Feel. You will only regret it if you don't." The redhead smiled softly at her.

"I think I may have misjudged you, Serena. I thought that you were, well…."

"A bitch?" Jackson and Serena answered at the same time.

Serena chuckled. "I can be. However, I should not have acted the way I did when we first met. Julius and I had just had a little spat that really had absolutely nothing to do with you."

"I was going to say you were out to get me. I really try to save that other word for people who truly deserve it." Lyssa smiled at her and was surprised to find herself laughing. "Serena, why didn't you know what I was thinking?"

"Because I, unlike some of the others here, try to give people their privacy. Speaking of which, Hunter?"

Lyssa was not surprised to hear his voice behind the door. "I'm going."

Lyssa sighed dramatically again. "Is it really hard to understand why I might need some space?" It was not like she did not want to be around him. Yes, she did find herself completely attracted to him, and they had been spending more time together. Hunter had not attempted to push the issue with her since the day he had kissed her.

"My dear, you must understand that your face has haunted Hunter for years now. He's been searching for you."

"That's so sad." Lyssa could not help but feel sorry for the time he had wasted.

"That's a little creepy. It's like he was stalking you before he even found you." Jackson shook his head as if to shake away something distasteful.

"It's not like that, Jackson. I told you about the locket. I saw my life with him. I am connected to him in ways I can't explain. There is no rhyme or reason to it." For once, Lyssa did not want to explain herself. There was a huge part of her that wanted to chase away any doubt that circled around her. She wanted to fall hopelessly in love without worrying about the consequences. Why did everything always have to be so damned complicated? Would it kill her to just let go for a change? Hadn't she earned that right with the crap she had dealt with in this life already?

"Why would that be creepy? I think it's adorable. I know it does seem strange, Jackson. But his soul will always love her. You'll understand it when you meet your soul mate too." Serena put a hand on Lyssa's arm.

"Serena, he doesn't really know her. He loves the idea of her."

"Jackson's right. What if I am not the woman he loved before? I'm probably nothing like her. Every life is different.

What if he wasted his time? What if there is someone out there who would be so much better for him?" She was speaking from that empty part of herself, the part that did not feel worthy of being loved by anyone else.

"Well first of all, I don't buy that crap. I'll smack the stupid out of you if you keep that up. You are beautiful, smart, kind, and loving. Any man would be lucky to have you," Jackson fired back at her.

"Besides, Lyssa, you want him every bit as much as he wants you. You may not have known you were looking for him, but your soul always will. And Jackson's right, that self-depreciation stops now. Do you think I ever once thought to degrade myself?" Serena clucked her tongue and shook her head at her.

"But you're...."

"What, beautiful? Of course I am. Do you want to know why? Because I stopped hiding in the corner you keep stuffing yourself into. You haven't had anyone take you under their wing before, have you? Looks like I have a lot more to teach you than I thought. Don't worry, Serena will provide."

Before she knew it, Serena had grabbed onto both of their hands and they were careening through the air. Lyssa yanked her arm away from her when they touched solid ground. "Where are we now?"

"Just you wait. All in good time." Serena sniffed the air once, then pulled on her hand before walking out of the alley they were standing in. Lyssa and Jackson followed behind her easily. She had left her wand at home, but she was sure that Serena had her back. Besides, it was daylight out. The shadows usually preferred the cloak of night.

They walked down the sidewalk, and she could see different shops around her. Lyssa was surprised when Serena stopped before a beauty salon called Classic Clips. Still confused as to her intent, she followed Serena into the shop.

"Time for a makeover, my dear."

"Oh, goodie!" clapped Jackson.

Lyssa tried to wave them both away, but Serena would have none of it. She pushed her into a seat and told her to wait there. When she returned, she brought a stylist with her. "See that girl there? Lots of hottie potential, right?"

As the stylist looked her over, Lyssa felt uncomfortable in her skin. Lyssa wanted to object to the scrutiny, but when the woman gave Serena a confident smirk, she knew she would easily be outvoted. "You're right about that. Add a few layers here and there, maybe some high and low lights."

"Definitely." Jackson crossed his arms, raised his eyebrows and said, "Well?"

"Fine."

As they fussed over her in the chair, she refused to look to see what they were doing. Lyssa had never really cared about the style of her hair before. What would one hair cut possibly accomplish? It was all inconsequential, because she would still be the same person she always was. But today was a new day, with new beginnings, so Lyssa decided not to worry about the moment and just let it all go.

"And don't forget the nails," Lyssa added halfway into her haircut. "They're hideous."

"That's the spirit!" Serena patted her on the back. It was nice to have her friends fuss over her. She was surprised Jackson wasn't turning cartwheels in the salon to show his exuberance.

While Beth, the stylist, was putting various foils in her hair, another lady was filing her nails. When the color was setting, her nails were finished up with a French manicure. The ladies showed her how to keep them shaped nicely, and put together a bag of things to take home with her to keep them pretty. Lyssa wondered how in the world they were paying for this, but when this thought popped into her head, Serena waved her hands at her to suggest that she need not worry about such things. She let out a deep sigh of relief and just enjoyed the attention.

When Beth turned her chair to face the mirror, she almost gasped out loud. The woman in the mirror looked nothing like her. The change was so startling, she almost forgot who she was. Lyssa found it hard to believe that she was staring at herself, but she knew it was her, still hardened on the inside, but softer on the edges. Once long stringy hair had been transformed into soft, flowing tresses that hit her face at different angles. There was no way she would ever be able to hide behind her hair again. The colors were so different than she was used to, and while they were unusual, they actually fit her quite well. A dark brown layer on the bottom was considered low lights, and she had blonde and red highlights that contrasted with her natural color. Instead of the dull brown that she had always hated, there was more of a warm chocolate brown mixed in now. Every time she swished her hair around her head, she felt like she saw a different color.

As she sat there, she saw something else that she had never seen before. Bright lights were emanating from all around her. She knew instantly what it was: her aura. Lyssa had never been able to see it before. It was almost as if she had set the colors inside herself free, and they were broadcasting for the world to see.

"Wow."

"That's right, Lyssa. Wow. You're gorgeous. Thank you ladies. See you next week at the meet up. Let's go, Lyssa."

"But don't we have to pay?" They may use magical currency to survive, but the rest of the world did not know that. It worked just the same as regular money.

Serena laughed quietly. "Did you notice the number on their wrists?"

Now that she mentioned it, Lyssa had seen the number 30 on Beth's left wrist, but she had not made the connection. "Are they Guardians?"

"Yep. Hiding among the rest of the world. They thrive on showing hidden beauty to the world, and since you are a guardian now, you get their best prices. The next place will not be free. Now, time for a wardrobe update." Serena pulled a credit card out of her pocket and smiled at her.

"Is that real?"

"Of course...not." Serena winked at her and put the card back in her purse. "But it works just as well as our money. A perk of being a guardian. You can't keep this fabulousness going without a little help." Serena put a hand on her hip and touched her hair with the other.

Lyssa stifled a giggle, unsure how to react to her outrageousness. Jackson poked her in the side and gave her a bright smile. It was clear that he was enjoying himself. Lyssa smacked his hand away and followed Serena into the nearest clothing shop.

Jackson and Serena both picked out a handful of tops, paired up with jeans that were a little too tight for her liking. Her wardrobe of choice made it easier to hide her insecurity with her body, for baggie clothing hid some of the curvy places that were out of control. Serena must have caught on to her thought process, for she shook her sassy head and told her that she needed to quit hiding them. So there she stood in front of a mirror in jeans that were almost hard to breathe in, with a white cotton shirt with quarter length sleeves. It had a v-neck with buttons that went down her chest. Jackson suggested she leave the top three buttons open for extra sex appeal.

"Who am I trying to attract?" Did she really need to attract Hunter's attention any more?

"Just keeping up with the thought that you are not the woman he knew, Lyssa. There's something much more inside you. It's just time for you to figure out what it is. No more hiding."

Lyssa glanced at the mirror again. Serena was right. No more hiding in the corners. No more hand-me downs. These clothes were meant for her, and for the first time, when she looked in the mirror, she did not despise her curves. And while she'd thought her aura could not change any more, she was mistaken. It was like a rainbow of light had surrounded her. Her eyes were open as wide as they could be…the two blue eyes in the middle of her face, as well as the third eye that was invisible to the rest of the world. Lyssa was awakening in ways that she had never expected, and if the rest of the world did not notice, then they were blind. Did that mean she should be reckless? It was tempting…she was not ready to throw all caution to the wind, but she was ready to live.

When they were finished shopping, Jackson teleported back to the apartment to study, and Lyssa followed Serena back to the Watch Tower. Lyssa turned to Serena and put a hand on her arm. "Serena, you promised to help me learn to block my thoughts. If I am to appear as confident as you say I should, then people should not be able to read the uncertainty echoing inside my head."

Serena led her through some breathing exercises to start her off. Then she had her do some visualizations.

"It's like your mind is a treasure chest. You have to make sure the lock is held tight before you encounter others. Only you can hold the key to open it. It sounds easier than it is, really. It just takes time. Give it a try."

Closing her eyes, she took a deep, calming breath. Lyssa envisioned the lid closing and the key turning in the lock. When she opened her eyes, she looked over at Serena. "Ask me something, and see if you can read the answer."

"What is your favorite color?"

Lyssa safely thought the word purple and waited to see if Serena would guess it. "Well?"

"Nada."

"Are you trying?"

"Yes. You're locked up tight, sweetie. Keep it up, and you should find yourself feeling a little safer around the rest of the group. It's always good to have some privacy."

"Thank you, Serena!" Lyssa could actually feel her smile brighten up her face. Yes, it was a brand new day indeed.

Elissa Daye

Chapter 12

As she waited for Hunter in the parlor of the Watch Tower, she could not help the thoughts that were racing through her head. Serena had brought up a valid point. Did she have real feelings for Hunter? Was there such a thing as love at first sight, or was this more of an attraction? Even though they had spent more time together on campus and at the Watch Tower, she had not known him long enough to be sure. Her past life memories were still buried deep below the surface. Perhaps it was the universe's way of saying that not every life has to repeat the exact same cycle. Hunter seemed comfortable basing his emotions on a memory, but she felt he was just in love with a faded photograph. If only it were that easy. Lyssa may not have had the emotional freedom he did, but what she did feel was enough to make her want to move further. Lyssa wanted to leap before looking for a change, instead of using the level head that ruled most of her life. She was infinitely curious about where this was going to take them, and hopeful that something good might actually come of it.

If she tried to diagnose her current state, she would find one thing to be true; her heart fluttered in her chest every time Hunter walked into the room. His dedication to saving the world around him was certainly admirable. One night they had taken a walk on the quad, and he had bent down to look at one of the rabbits that was watching them both cautiously. Hunter had spoken to it softly and tried to coax it nearer. A little piece of her heart melted that night. How many men felt comfortable enough with their manhood to have a one-sided conversation with a wild animal where anyone walking by could see? He was an original, one of a kind, and even if she had not had some preconceived memory of him, part of her would have been drawn to him. It certainly would be easy to fall for him completely, if only she knew it was her that he wanted, the one that existed in the here and now.

"Lyssa? You look amazing. Are you ready to go?" When Hunter continued through the doorway, he paused and took another long lingering glance at her.

She cleared her throat and made sure her thoughts were on lock down before she answered. "Sure. Where to?"

"My favorite place." Hunter grabbed her hand, and they were instantly transported to a place she had never been before.

"Where are we?" Staring out into the distance, she could see a valley of red rocks and sand below her. The mystery of the moment overwhelmed her, for it felt as if she could see another lifetime rolling through the valley below them. It was quiet, but it was haunting at the same time, as the dry winds blew calmly around them. Lyssa felt trapped in a moment in time, a memory of a world long forgotten, where the wagon trains wheeled in between the rocky summits. She had never been to anywhere filled with so much nostalgia before.

"You feel that too, don't you? We're in the Badlands."

"South Dakota? Seriously? I've never been here before. It's peaceful. Still." Lyssa sat down on the bench overlooking the bluffs and crossed her feet under her. "I could stay here for hours."

Hunter looked at her and smiled. "I know the feeling."

"Hunter, do you see the images of the past down in those valleys? It's like watching a caravan pull through the hills. Amazing."

"I knew you'd see it too. You're so perceptive to spiritual imprints." He turned back to look down in the valley.

Lyssa was surprised that Hunter wanted to bring her here. Up until this point, they had only spent time together on campus or at the Watch Tower. Now that they were here, he simply sat next to her. They talked about common interests outside of the Watch Tower. She wanted to know more about who Hunter was before he joined the Guardians.

"I was actually just starting college before I got the call. I had just chosen my major. I've always felt a kinship with animals, so veterinary science seemed like the best choice. Julius recruited me."

"Were you practicing magic at the time?"

"Yes. I was practicing healing, among other things. I wanted to bring holistic healing into my work, healing animals with natural remedies."

"That explains that calm healing energy I feel when I'm around you. I bet you'll be a fantastic vet."

"I hope so, but my work as a guardian will always come first."

Lyssa smiled at him. "I love animals. I always wanted a cat, but we couldn't afford a pet. Then, when I moved away from home, I got so caught up in forgetting my past that I just wanted to be free, more than anything."

"I'm glad you found yourself."

"I'm not quite what you expected, I'm sure." She smiled up at him and pushed a lock of hair behind her ears.

"I'm not grading you on a memory, Lyssa."

"Hmmm?" She was pretending to stare down at the valley below.

"Yes, you may have been in my past, but the person you are in this life is not the one you were then. I'm not the same either."

"But you said you loved her. That you were looking for her again."

"At first, I was. Not anymore."

"Oh." She tried not to sound disappointed. Perhaps he had decided that she wasn't what he was looking for after all. "I get it. It's okay." Lyssa closed her eyes and tried not to let the moment of silence destroy her. Yes, she was already in way too deep.

She felt Hunter shift next to her, and when she looked up he was standing.

"Don't look at me like that." His eyes were almost burning through her, and it made her shake almost nervously.

"Like what?" His smoky eyes searched hers for her meaning.

"I don't know. I've never had anyone look at me like that." Lyssa looked away uncomfortably. Why did she feel so skittish all of a sudden? During the confusion, her guard over her thoughts fell.

"Lyssa, you misunderstood." He sat back down, pulled her close to him, and made her look into his eyes. "It's not a memory I want. I want you."

She could feel the heat of his breath on her lips right before he kissed her. The kiss lasted a lifetime before they came up for air. Bringing her hand up to his face, she pulled him down for another kiss. The urge to hide from him would no longer rule her. She was more awake now than she had ever been. When the kiss ended, she put her head on his shoulder and tried to catch her breath. Lyssa inhaled his scent and closed her eyes. This was much more than where she wanted to be. It was where she needed to be, for however long it lasted. If she lost him in the end, at least she would have his memory to hold onto. The journey would be worth it.

They stood there on that ridge for another hour as they traded kisses and caresses that took her breath away hours later. When she returned to the apartment, her heart was still beating rapidly. Her body was certainly awake, and she knew she would have let him go much further, but Hunter did not want to rush things between them. She agreed. It was nice to take things slow and enjoy each moment together.

Elissa Daye

Chapter 13

For the next few weeks, when Lyssa was not studying or training at the Watch Tower, she spent her free time with Hunter. Jackson constantly teased her when she came home with a flushed face, but she laughed it off. While he did not completely understand the dynamics of her relationship with Hunter, Jackson had resolved to be supportive.

Lyssa was soon becoming a mess of pent up energy, for while they always separated each night before things went too far, it left her body aching, for what she did not quite know. How in the world was Hunter dealing with it?

All her extra energy was put into her training at the Watch Tower and learning how to locate the shadows through astral projection. It was imperative that her ethereal tether remained intact each time she traveled to a new area. The trick was to get there without being detected. Once there, her spirit walked over the area, searching for the shadows she had detected. In many cases, it was deserted houses and buildings. These beings were not the typical shadows she had seen before…these only seemed to cause trouble to those people who dared to enter. Finding a better way of shadow detection was essential, especially for the ones that rose from the Land of the Shadows to destroy human life. Once she could do this with more accuracy, then she would be more helpful to her sector.

While she had been doing a lot of studying, she had also been on daily hunts with Julius. They were taking down more shadows together every day. Sometimes they took Jackson with them, but for the most part, Julius wanted her to learn how to defend herself, so that if none of them were available, she would still be able to take care of herself. Lyssa had learned how to create a shield of light around her, so that anything the shadows sent her way would rebound off her. She was working on mastering her wand skills, and added new spells to her repertoire at the same time.

Trying to accomplish in a short period of time what had taken others a lifetime was not easy. If she'd had the years of training that others had, she would not feel so inadequate. From what she understood, when Julius and Serena had been taken under the Watch Tower's wings, they had needed to complete at least two years worth of training before they were put into the field. However, times were changing, and the members of the Craven were finding ways to open more portals for the shadows to enter their world each day.

Hunter and Logan were doing the best they could to infiltrate the Craven. The Craven was not as wide and extensive as the Watch Tower, but it was growing. Their need to destroy the world made them a danger to everything the guardians held dear. Every single day, she worried that Hunter might not return. They were both trying to join the ranks of the Craven so that they could understand how they worked and figure how to take them down with the least amount of casualties. She only hoped that whatever darkness they kept around them did not taint Hunter or Logan.

Hunter and Logan had just given them an update about what they had learned so far. The Craven was a group of people who dealt with the darkest parts of magic, essentially the complete opposite of the Watch Tower. They seemed to gain more power from the shadows that they had set loose on the world. They were like vampires, feeding on the energy of those around them and controlling those that were too weak to fend them off. Hunter said he had watched as one of the Craven had used his powers of persuasion to artfully make a woman break into another person's house, just to see if he could. This man had used his psychic powers of suggestion to put an impulse into her head, and watched from afar as the woman followed his orders. He had gotten a good laugh as he watched her confusion as the cops had carried her away.

The other thing that they had been able to report was the Cravens' ability to siphon energy out of unsuspecting people. Their favorite places to gather were restaurants, grocery stores, and movie theatres...basically any place that a lot of people gathered. They would go into these places with their wands hidden under their long black trench coats and wait for discord to erupt around them. People started pushing their carts like they were in the Indy 500, disregarding the people around them, and glaring at anyone intruding in their space, as if they had no right to be in their way. This energy festered like an infected wound in front of them, and they siphoned it directly into the crystals they also carried with them. These crystals, when charged, were used in rituals to open more portals for the shadows to enter their world.

Their relationship with the shadows was more than symbiotic. It allowed them to create a vortex of energy that grew rapidly around the world. This vortex would one day split the world in half and define the line between what was good and evil so clearly that the world would never be the same. A perpetual loss of balance would start, and these entities would find a way to tear their world apart. The guardians needed to find a way to weaken both the Craven and the shadows so that this never came to pass.

Lyssa was in her room reading one of the books from the library, hoping to find a clue that would help them, when her left arm started to tingle. Her tattoo was changing colors, the summons making it clear that something was up. She set the book on her bed and teleported to the library.

When she arrived there, the others were already gathered around the table. Hunter's gaze penetrated her. He had not seen her since lunch earlier. She closed her eyes quickly and imagined the key turning in her head to lock out his probing questions. Locking it up at all times might be wise, but it took effort to do so, and sometimes she just wanted to relax. She looked back over at him and saw the small mischievous smile light up his face.

Lyssa looked over at Julius. "What's going on?"

"The Craven are up to no good. I'm afraid your city may be in trouble."

Hunter, Jackson, and Lyssa all exchanged glances. "So what exactly are they up to, Julius? What makes this different?" Lyssa suddenly worried that Lana might be in danger. She had kept up with Lana the best that she could with her hectic schedule, but it seemed like she hadn't talked to her for a little while. Guilt ate at her conscience, and Lyssa knew she would have to make it a point to check in with her soon.

"As you know, the shadows are always present. The guardians are only concerned when there are too many present in any one area. In your town, the Craven near you seem to be summoning them forward at a faster rate than other areas. The guardians have known there are many cells of the Craven. Hunter and Logan are infiltrating this cell to see what they can learn. These shadows are not just seeping from the ground slowly, as they are in other places. There has to be a new portal somewhere."

"What do you suggest, Julius?" Logan asked him. Logan had always seemed so innocent, but the fire burning in his eyes right then showed exactly the opposite.

"First we find them." Julius looked over at her, and she knew that he was waiting for her to say something.

"I can do that. I've done it before. I can show you where they were the last time I saw them, but what are we going to do when we find them?"

Hunter looked extremely concerned. It was clear that he did not want her to put herself at risk. Anyone looking at him could tell he was fighting a battle with himself.

Lyssa took a deep breath. "I can do this, Hunter."

"If I lose her again...."

"Hunter, stop. This is bigger than all of us." Lyssa stood up and reached over to the globe in front of them. She remembered the night when she had used her animal guide to help her find the shadows. When she looked down, the globe displayed a city map, and she pointed to where the warehouse was located on Main Street. "Here. But they are not there at the moment. The last time I tried, it was later in the evening, if you recall. It's still early."

"Is that where the portal is?" Julius asked her quickly.

"No." Somehow, she just knew that the portal had to be somewhere else. The Craven had summoned something out of the fire before, but that was not a shadow, especially if it was surrounded by the light like that. It had to be somewhere else. "But I know I can find it. Give me a few minutes." Lyssa had been practicing all those long hours for this very thing. All she had to do was give it a chance. It would come.

Putting her hands at both ends of the map of the city, she kept each one just an inch away from the surface. Her fingertips roamed all over the map on the globe, waiting to feel the warm energy she usually felt when she was locating the shadows. This time, it would be more difficult, because she was looking for a portal that would probably only give off residual energy.

"Here." A faint tingling feeling had passed from the map to her fingertips. There was some kind of vortex...this had to be it.

"We move."

Lyssa could see the place she wanted to move to in the forefront of her mind. Closing her eyes, she willed her body to move through time and space. In an instant, she was standing at the entrance to a graveyard with the other four.

"Figures," muttered Logan. Jackson covered a laugh with a cough and Lyssa jabbed him in the side with her elbow. She put a hand on Logan's shoulder. Logan was actually younger than her. While he had more training with the Watch Tower, he still felt very much like a younger brother. The idea of him attempting to join the Craven to spy behind the scenes nibbled on her conscience. They might eat him alive. She did not like Hunter attempting it either, but she knew if it was her choice to do the same, Hunter would not be able to keep her from it. They each had to do what was necessary to protect the world.

As far as graveyards went, this one was not particularly exceptional. For the most part, it was peaceful and calm. Most people expected to find spirits crossing from one end to the other, but spirits were more attached to places they had frequented when they were living. How many people liked to spend their time on Earth at a cemetery? Perhaps a caretaker or gravedigger here or there, but very few others would want to reside within its walls. People were usually just spooked by the idea that there were bodies buried under the ground. She always laughed any time she saw a paranormal investigation group trying to find paranormal activity near graves, for they often left with no evidence of paranormal activity.

There was one road leading into the cemetery. To the right was a caretaker's house that was used as a sort of guard station during the day. The person who took care of this place took pride in the work done there. The grass was well tended, for its green blades had just been trimmed, as proven by the sweet smell of the pollen in the air. The trees that she could see from the entrance were healthy, and each sported a fair amount of leaves for late spring.

They walked the winding road that separated the graves from one side to the other. When she felt energy pulling her, she led the group to the back corner of the western side of the graveyard. There were several unmarked tombstones in this area, which she found slightly unusual. Were these bodies that had been relinquished to the county coroner?

When she looked to the grave farthest away from the road, she felt a chill go up her spine. While the rest of the grass had appeared green in the cemetery, the color of this grass ranged from yellow to light brown. The tree three feet away from the gravestone was unlike any of the other trees. It held no leaves at all, and the way that it twisted and turned toward the sky made it appear like a deadly hand grasping for…what, she could only guess. Her guide, Jephilia, was standing next to the tree and pointing at the headstone of the grave. She gestured to the others to stay where they were as she walked over to find out what else she could tell her.

"You must be careful, Lyssa. The portal is open and active. The shadows can emerge at any point. If you choose to enter the portal, I cannot guarantee your safety. I'm unable to follow you there. You may not be able to return if you are caught. I can sense so many uncertainties lay within its depths. Be careful."

"Thank you, Jephilia. You know we must go. We need to find out as much as we can about their world so that we may protect ours."

Jephilia nodded at her before disappearing. Her guide had done her job for now. She knew that she would not be able to stop Lyssa from entering. Jephilia understood her better than she understood herself sometimes.

"Jephilia says to be careful. The shadows can come at any time. If we are sensed, the shadows will be doing whatever they can to stop us from escaping. We'll have to be ready to teleport out at any time."

When she walked closer to the gravestone, she could feel that the air was colder right behind the headstone than anywhere else around it. She closed her eyes and concentrated on opening her third eye. When she opened her eyes, she could see a large circle of energy that was swarming in front of her. This was the portal, for it was only visible to magical eyes. Lyssa turned to look at the others and gestured for them to come closer.

"Do you see that?" she asked them.

"I feel it more than I see it," Jackson answered her.

Lyssa could see a slight shiver go through Logan. "We have to go in, don't we?"

Julius answered for her. "It's inevitable, Logan. We have to see what we are up against. If the shadows gain their power from the Land of the Shadows, then we must see for ourselves what is fueling them."

"Actually, Julius, I think that since Hunter and Logan are trying to find a way into the Craven, perhaps they should sit the rest of this mission out," Serena suggested.

"She's right." Lyssa could not help but agree with her. Clearly, it did not earn her points with Hunter at the moment. His eyes showed that he was not very happy with her words.

"What if you need me?"

"Hunter, if I need you, you will know." She was sure of that, more sure than she had been in a long time. He would hear her if she called out for him.

"Fine. But we're waiting here until you come out."

It was agreed that only four of them would be entering the portal. She felt shivers go up her spine as she got closer to the entrance, and while part of her courage was failing, she knew she had to go through it. Closing her eyes, she stepped forward. As she walked through the portal, she could feel the space around her changing drastically. It was as if she went from one season to the other within seconds. It was all sunshine and light breezes on her side of the world, but inside the portal, it was almost like a frigid wind was roaring around her. When she made it through the portal, the climate evened out. She waited for the others to step in behind her.

"What is this, a cave?"

"I don't know, Serena. It's so dark in here that it's hard to see anything. Should we light our wands?" Lyssa really did not like the pitch black around them. It would be a lot easier if they could light a wand to see their way through this place.

"I don't trust it," Jackson interjected.

"Agreed. We'll have to wait for our eyes to adjust. From here, we will need to mindspeak. If there is anyone watching this area, they could hear us," Julius answered.

Lyssa wanted to add that if there was anything in this place, chances were they could already see them, as their eyes were made for this darkness. It seemed pointless to point that out though. Besides, she could not feel any shadows near them.

It was almost five minutes before she could see where she was stepping. They were moving down what appeared to be a tunnel, or a long, narrow cave. After walking for a few minutes, she could see a dim light coming from ahead.

"*Do you see the light?*" She turned towards Julius.

"*Yes. We'll need to be very careful here.*" He nodded his head towards the light, and they gathered together. From there on, she did not want to be the one in the lead. As far as she was concerned, the other two were more prepared for an attack than she was, for her strengths were identifying and understanding energy around her. It was a natural ability for her. Julius took the lead, and Serena took the flank, leaving her and Jackson in the middle.

When they turned the corner, they were staring at what looked like an old subway entrance. Did the shadows' world have a subway? Lyssa felt slightly intrigued. She wondered what else they had. They walked down the tunnel until they found concrete stairs leading up to the world above them. It was weird to have entered a portal that took them underneath their world, only to be heading up to somewhere that none of them really knew.

Julius turned towards her. "*What do you sense ahead of us?*"

"*Quiet. Solitude. No shadows at the moment. We should be safe.*" Lyssa closed her eyes and made herself focus really hard on the stairs ahead of them. They walked up the stairs quietly with their wands at the ready. When they could see out of the stairway into the world, they gazed over the top of the stairs.

The sight that met their eyes was entirely unexpected. The land resembled a metropolitan area, much like any city she had seen before. Some of the buildings were slightly demolished, others were completely intact, but no sign of life permeated the area. Black ashes rained down on the world, and it looked very much like a snow globe with tarnished flakes. It was as if the whole world had never discovered Technicolor. Everything in the Land of Shadows was cast in shades of gray scale, ranging from white all the way to black.

Jackson looked over at Julius. *"Are we going up there?"*

Lyssa was glad that Jackson had asked the question, so that she did not have to. They were just sitting there, and she could not sense anything, but waiting for something to happen did not seem very smart. Why chance fate? After all, they were as much a target hiding in this stairwell as they would be above ground.

Julius looked at her. *"What do you feel up there?"*

She closed her eyes and shut out all the static around her. Once again, she tried to see if she felt any energy up there that she would consider a threat. *"At the moment, we are shadow free. If we wait here in one spot for too long, they may sense us. We need to keep moving."*

Julius was the first to climb the last step up from the subway. They followed closely behind him. There would always be safety in numbers, especially in a world they had never been in before. Continuing carefully, they walked a few blocks before they heard the cries. Someone down here was in considerable pain. While they were intruders to this world, it was still not in their nature to let anyone suffer needlessly.

Lyssa pulled a pencil and a piece of paper out of the small backpack and started sketching quickly. She drew all the buildings around them and put the pencil down. Running her fingers over the drawings, she knew that she had pinpointed where the cries were coming from when she touched the tallest building on the other side of the street. All the practice that she been forced to do in the past few weeks made it easier to trust her instincts.

"There. That building. We'll need to go quickly. It doesn't sound like we have much time if we're going to help."

The others were in agreement with her. They moved quickly across the street, not really watching where they were going, because all of the cars were old, rusted, and definitely not moving an inch. Every once in a while, they saw the black shadow of a bird fly across the sky, but the shadow people were nowhere to be found. Did that mean that they were above ground? Would it be considered above ground, if they had just come up from somewhere that had been under them in their world? Was this Land of the Shadows really underneath the ground they walked on, or was it a dimension somewhere else? Lyssa wondered why no one had ventured here before. She decided now was as good a time as any to ask.

"Are we the first to travel here?"

"Through that portal, yes. Others have been through other portals, but few have lived to tell what they have seen." Julius refused to look at her.

"Are you freaking kidding me? So what you're saying is we may not return?" Jackson shook his head in disbelief.

"If Lyssa keeps her shadow detection going, we should be fine, Jackson. So, please let her focus. It could mean the difference between life and death."

Hunter must have known what they were getting into down here. That explained the darkened expression on his face when they had moved closer to the portal. She had learned another lesson today though: always ask for more details before she followed Julius anywhere. As far as leaders go, he really did not think to prepare them with all the knowledge that they needed before they moved forward. This made her think he must still be new at this role. She couldn't help thinking that perhaps they needed new management.

Lyssa realized her thoughts were wandering, and once again tried to focus on the task at hand. They had just entered the building and could hear the screams from the bottom of the stairs. The guardians climbed up one step at a time and stopped on the third floor when Julius put a hand up to listen for the screams again. When they heard them this time, they realized there was more than one of them coming from the fourth floor just above them. They climbed the last flight of stairs leading to the fourth floor.

The door opened to a large open space. She had almost expected to see a hallway leading to other doors they would have to maneuver through. When she glanced across the room, a dozen people were sitting on the floor against the back wall, except they were no longer people…they were not corporeal at all. Their images were projections of what they must have looked like in life; it was easy to see through them. They were the same gray scale color as the rest of this world. Each one seemed to be plagued by some horror that she could not see. She did not see anything physically holding them in place, except a long black string of smoke that acted as a spiritual anchor that locked them to the ground, like a dark black chain of smoke had attached to them.

"*Their souls are trapped here.*" Serena shook her head sadly.

"*Is there anything we can do to help them?*" Lyssa hated to see these souls trapped here in such a fashion. No one deserved to spend their afterlife in this pain.

Before anyone could answer, there was a loud movement below them in the streets. She ran to the window and looked out. The shadows were swarming below, almost as if they sensed the guardians' life energies within their walls, but these were not like the shadows they usually saw. They were moving like an infantry, and their shapes no longer hovered over the ground. Their shapes were clearly formed, and when they moved, each step could be heard. These shadows had gained almost enough energy to take on physical form.

Every inch of her knew why these souls were tethered in agony in the Land of the Shadows. The shadows were draining the rest of the light from them and forming their own corporeal shapes. The way they existed on their world had never been physical. Their powers over people were more of mental persuasion from afar. The shadows above could not physically alter or change a person at all. These shadows were certainly more of a threat and would probably have a greater power over a person's thoughts as they fed off their unsuspecting victims. It was clear that a new regiment of shadows was a deadly threat to the guardians' world. She prayed that these shadows never left the Land of the Shadows to walk upon their Earth.

Lyssa turned to the souls trapped within the room and took a chance. "Where did you come from?" she asked one aloud. At first, the woman in front of her was still transfixed in a place where she could not reach her. Pulling out her wand, Lyssa sent all her warmest energy into the black chains surrounding her. They started to shake and rattle around the woman. It was enough to get her attention. Lyssa looked at her, and asked her again. "Where did you come from?"

"Chicago. The windy city."

Good. She was lucidly answering her. "What happened to you?"

"I couldn't eat or sleep. All I wanted to do was die. It was easier that way, at least that is what the voices told me."

This spirit must have killed herself in some shape or form. "Why did your spirit not move on?"

"The shadows took me before I could rise up. They brought me down. I've been here ever since."

There was the sound of steps coming up the stairs. "Lyssa, we have to go now!" Julius shouted at her.

Lyssa wanted to free the souls before her, but Julius was right, she had to leave now. If she was the one who could find the shadows in their sector, then she had to make sure she got out. Without lingering further, she closed her eyes, took a deep breath, and imagined the Watch Tower in her mind. It took her a little longer to get there than she wanted, but she knew the Watch Tower was cleansing her aura before it would allow her to enter. This cleansing was a safety net, so that if anything chose to follow her, her psychic scent or energy would be lost to them.

Lyssa stood in the library and held her breath. She only hoped the other three made it out unharmed as well. Within a few minutes, the rest of them appeared before her. "You guys okay?"

"What were you doing, Lyssa?" Julius started in on her right away.

"We need answers, Julius. We could have waited there forever in silence, but it would not have helped us figure out what we really came there to find out." Lyssa crossed her arms and returned his scowl.

"She's right, Julius. We found out something important today. Those things are trapping their victims from our world and feeding off their souls. We can't allow this to continue." Jackson came readily to her defense.

"What happens if they get enough tortured souls to rise up from the ground with the physical forms we just saw? Will they be able to do more to us than control the thoughts of others? Will they be able to physically harm others? We have to stop as many of them as we can. The Watch Tower cannot allow the shadows to feed off the innocent anymore." Lyssa could foresee many different scenarios if this came to pass, all of them ending in desolation that they could only prevent if they took action now.

At first, Julius did not answer her. His look of irritation left slowly from his face and was replaced with a pensive frown. "We have to start with the Craven. They are providing too many portals for these shadows. It's imperative that we cut off their access. Once we do this, they will have fewer ways to feed on our people."

Lyssa did not add that they would eventually need to go back to free the souls of the ones they had lost. They all knew they had to do something, but the guardians had to start with what they could accomplish first. It would not happen as swiftly as they would like it to, but it would happen. They had to inform the other sectors about this new information as well.

Chapter 14

After talking to Julius and Serena, she went home for the night. There were so many thoughts swarming around in her mind, like brittle locusts that crawled intermittently. What she really needed was time to think. Lyssa knew their goal was to keep the shadows away from their world, but she could not help feeling that they should also be focusing on providing assistance to the souls that were trapped in the Land of the Shadows. She had almost been a casualty of the power of the shadows. If her spirit guide had not come forth to speak with her, would she still be standing there right now? Or would she have been tethered to the ground with no hope for escaping the darkness that filled all her days with a helpless void? Would she have survived the sad delusions that eroded her soul? She would like to think so, but she was a different person now than she had been even a month ago. Lyssa no longer dwelled on the past that had cut her so deeply…her anger no longer sliced into her every waking moment. It no longer fed the person that she was. She had a higher purpose, and she felt that those souls trapped with the darkness below them deserved the right to ascend to their higher purpose. How could those people ever be reborn if they were trapped there? Lyssa would definitely be pushing this issue as soon as they had struck down the Craven.

How does one attack another human? The thought did not settle well with her. It never really had. Does one destroy another's life to preserve hundreds of others? Would it be possible to destroy their powers without destroying them? There were those who studied magic who believed that a person's powers could be bound with little harm to the individual. To do this, they would need more information about the people they were up against. The only way for this to work was for Hunter and Logan to infiltrate them. She hated the danger that surrounded Hunter every time he left the Watch Tower to continue his pretense. He could be caught at any moment; if he were, would he be able to escape?

Sometimes she wished that she could be helping with the infiltration, that she could blend in as easily with their foe, but it was not meant to be. The Watch Tower needed her here. Every sector of guardians had someone with the ability to scan energy to locate whatever foe they were fighting against. She knew the Craven must have this skill too, for when she had used her animal spirit to project to where they were, they had easily detected her energy gleaming off the raven, for she had not learned how to utilize stealth. Within minutes, they had followed the trail of energy and pinpointed her location. They had not been pleased that she had been able to locate them. At least she had learned from that experience. Now when she went out, she was sure to cloak her signals to cover any imprint she left, since they had already found her once. That, and she never traveled alone.

Lyssa was so caught up in her thoughts that she had not heard the knock on the door. She turned around when the door swung open. Hunter was standing there with the most serious look that she had ever seen. "Why didn't you answer?"

"I'm sorry. I was lost in thought. I didn't hear you." It was easy to see that Hunter was worried about her. "Don't worry. I'm here. In one piece."

"Jackson let me in. You never returned to the cemetery. I was worried about you after I talked to Julius. You have to be more careful, Lyssa."

"For someone throwing himself into the fray, do you really have the right to tell me what to do?" Lyssa should be irritated that he was trying to boss her around, but he truly was doing it out of regard for her safety. It was sweet…slightly grating, but mostly sweet.

"I do what I have to, Lyssa. You know that." His hands gestured helplessly in front of him.

She smiled up at him. "Relax. I know better than you think. I'm okay. If I had not spoken up, then how would we know that the shadows were growing in number and in strength by using these poor souls? I wish people would start to see how valuable I am. I am capable of more than just being a human satellite, Hunter."

Hunter crossed the room and reached out to touch her arm. "I do believe in you, Lyssa. I just want you to be careful."

"Ditto." She smiled up at him and let all the frustration leave her body. Lyssa did not like to hold onto any negative energy when Hunter was around. It was a bitter diatribe compared to the healing, peaceful energy that made Hunter who he was.

"That's better. There's the smile that I love."

Lyssa shook her head and swatted his arm away with her hand. If he wanted to start acting all googly-eyed on her, then she would not know what to do with herself. Yes, she cared very deeply about Hunter, and it could easily be classified as love, but she still did not find the teasing banter between a woman and man to be an easy thing to stomach. How did one learn to tease and flirt? Lyssa had never really had the time to learn. With their future so deeply knitted in finding the shadows, she could not guarantee they would get much time together, but she would take whatever she could get.

"Would you like to go to our favorite place? Perhaps we need to meditate to shake off some of this energy."

It was not what she really wanted to do, but it was clear that being trapped within the confines of her bedroom might not be the wise thing to do at this point in time. Lyssa found herself making the safe choice and reached out for Hunter's hands, then teleporting to the small wooden bench overlooking the Badlands.

The scenery was much the same as it was before. The air was a little chillier tonight, so she snuggled closer to Hunter's side. He lifted up his arm and pulled her closer to him. It was nice to sit there with him, to just enjoy the calm around them. Words were left unspoken between them, for there was no need to say anything to enjoy the togetherness they shared.

Her mind wandered across various topics, one of them being her birthday, which was coming up soon, and that she had only spent it with Jackson in the past. She wondered what it would be like now that Hunter was in her life too. Would Jackson be upset if she wanted to spend the night out with Hunter instead? Of course, she hated to assume that Hunter would take her out, especially since she had not shared her birth date with him yet.

"All you had to do was ask," Hunter said with a quirky smile.

"I thought that was supposed to be up to the guy to do." Lyssa jabbed him in the ribs with her finger for reading her thoughts. Realizing he had read her mind, she quickly put her thoughts on lockdown and looked up at him.

"I have to be away for a few days, Lyssa. But when I return, we'll go out somewhere. We'll manage it. I promise. Jackson can always come along too."

Lyssa pulled out of his embrace and stood. She looked out over the valleys below them and felt the energy change. Something was not right. "Hunter, we need to leave at once. Before we're detected." They teleported back to the Watch Tower as quickly as possible.

"It wasn't me this time, Hunter. I think they were looking for you."

His gray eyes narrowed at her. "The Craven must have sent them to find me."

"Does that mean they are on to you?" Worry and a sinking dread churned in the pit of her stomach.

"No. It's the natural order of things. It's fine really. I promise."

Lyssa put her hands on his face and really looked at him. His thoughts were blocked from her, as usual. She felt like he was telling her the truth in this instance, but that there was also something else that he was not telling her. For now, she would have to be satisfied with the answer he had given her. It was one of the first nights that he walked away before kissing her good night. It did not sit well with her.

That night, she dreamt that the Craven had called Hunter home to roost. She could see him in the dimly lit room as the Craven nearest him beckoned him forward. She could see the man clearly. He was a large man, with a round head that appeared to be shaved close to the scalp, making his head look like a melon. The way his eyes squinted made him look very much like a cartoon mole. He was dressed in black from his head to his toes, and the only thing about him that made him seem menacing was the athame he held in his hand. Hunter bowed before the man, and when the man brought the athame up to Hunter's neck, she expected him to flinch, but he made no movement at all.

"Take this athame. You know what to do."

Hunter grabbed it and approached the box in the corner. He reached into it and pulled out a snake that was hissing at him fiercely. He held the snake down on a large overturned crate and sliced the athame through the air. She did not see what happened, for she woke up in a deep cold sweat. Lyssa felt the sorrow float on the air as part of Hunter died that night. This was not just a dream. The innocence that had circled around him so easily before would no longer be there. He would be plagued with the things that these Craven made him do, and yet he would do it for the greater good, to save the world from the horrors that would soon be on the way.

Chapter 15

Hunter never spoke of that night with her. He never even alluded to it in front of the others. He did tell them that he had passed an initiation and was now considered a full-fledged member of the Craven. Logan had passed his as well. From there, the men were doing what they could to help them pinpoint the movement of the Craven without it being obvious where the information was coming from. They all wanted to act on the information, but they knew that if they attacked them too early, it would reflect poorly on their undercover guardians, and while the mission was important, their people were important too.

Even though Hunter was extremely caught up in his mission, he remained true to his word. He made sure to fulfill her birthday requests. Lyssa spent the morning of her birthday with Jackson, reminiscing about every birthday they had ever spent together. When she explained that Hunter had offered to include him in their outing that evening, he declined with a smirk. Lyssa knew he did not want to be a third wheel. A small pang of regret filled her. She hadn't been spending as much time with him lately, certainly not as much as before they had become guardians. Both of them were balancing a normal life mixed in with their magical life, a task that wasn't easy. At least they got to spend some training time together.

Later that day, Hunter surprised her with a cake that he had made himself, then after singing "Happy Birthday" to her, he asked where she would like to go out that night. While the date started out well, after a while she was sitting by herself. They had moved together on the dance floor, but soon it became clear they were being watched. Lyssa had made sure to wear an amulet to mask her energy. No one knew her by her face, so they should have been safe.

Hunter, however, had not taken the same precautions. The Craven had followed him there, so he had to spend some time dealing with them so that they would not get suspicious. It was one of those moments where they said jump, and he asked how high. Lyssa knew that if they wanted to be able to find out the Cravens' initiatives that she had to let Hunter be for the moment. It did not help that it was her birthday, and here she was sitting alone at this bar. Twenty-two was a good year, right? She ordered herself a drink and was not at all surprised when she was carded. Lyssa looked much younger than she ever felt.

While she sat there listening to the music and sipping on her drink, she could feel the intrusive stares from the women nearest her. They had seen her with Hunter, and they were not even trying to hide their conversation from the rest of the world. Lyssa had never run into such catty people in her life.

"Can you believe that she was with him?" the blonde said to her black-haired friend.

"He probably felt sorry for her. He didn't stick around very long, did he?"

"Poor thing. She should know better than to set her sights so high."

They finally moved away, but their thoughts echoed in her head. She knew she should not buy into their petty remarks, but it was hard to counteract the thoughts that were bouncing around inside. Lyssa needed to drown out this negative energy; after all, it was her birthday, and she should be happy. Time to live it up a little.

"Bartender, I'll have another please."

She had finished off that one and another by the time Hunter came back to the bar. She was no longer thinking about the jealous words of the two women. When Hunter sat down next to her, all she could think about was the magnetic pull she felt every time she was near him. The feelings she got whenever he was around her had only started to get stronger.

"Do you want to dance?" Hunter reached his hand out for hers, and she took it.

"Are they gone?"

"Yes. They've gone. You have me all to yourself."

"Oh goodie." Lyssa looked away and tried not to grind her teeth.

"I'm sorry, Lyssa. I know it's your birthday. I had no idea—"

"It's okay, Hunter. I do understand." She turned to him and gave him a gentle smile. Lyssa really did understand. She also had given most of her life to the Watch Tower recently. At least she had made it more of a point to touch base with Lana. Apparently, her coven was experimenting with light to see if they could find a natural way to block the portals that allowed the shadows to enter the world. Lyssa had warned her to be careful not to be noticed, because the Craven would not be happy to find anyone interfering with their plans to fill the world with shadows.

Hunter tugged on her hand. "Well?"

"Why not?"

At first a fast paced song blared across the crowded room. She felt the beat of the drums pulse through her in a way that made her blood pressure rise. Dancing so close to

Hunter with these emotions running through her was almost more than she could take. When the blonde from earlier came very close to grinding on Hunter from behind, the little green eyed monster inside her almost shrieked at her, but the perceptive part of her knew that she did not have to worry about Hunter. His eyes were only on her, and when she swayed closer to him, she could feel the heartbeat in his chest as loudly as her own. She did not need anyone else to judge how beautiful or attractive she was. She could feel the effect they had on each other. No one could take away from that.

When a slow song started, she moved into his strong embrace and could feel his breath on her cheek. Lyssa tried hard to make her heart slow down, but her senses were extremely heightened from the drinks that she had finished off. It was not like she had never been tipsy before, she just had never let herself feel this free. There were no dark and depressing thoughts, no need to restrain herself any longer. There was just Hunter; his beautiful face, his strong body, and the scent of him, all of which were driving her crazy.

When she raised her head and tried to push away to distance herself just a little, she saw that Hunter was feeling the same magnetic force that she was. She pulled his face down to hers and started what was soon to become the first of many moments that would steal her breath away. Both of them were letting go of whatever had been holding them back. It was new, and there was a hint of danger in the energy that swarmed between them. They could be crossing a line they had not been willing to cross until now. Something had changed, and she could not pinpoint what exactly that was, but she no longer cared.

She could hear the disappointed voices of the catty women who had sat there with their glasses filled with judgment. It no longer fazed her. Turning toward them, she tilted her head haughtily and flipped her finger as Hunter and she were leaving the bar. It was delicious to hear the intake of breaths as they tried to look away from her. *Yes, eat your heart out ladies. He's all mine.*

"Hunter?" She looked up at him questioningly.

"Lyssa." He looked at her with eyes that he was trying very much to control. It was if he longed to say what his body cried out for, but was afraid to voice it to her.

"I know. I feel it too, Hunter. What are we going to do about it?" Lyssa felt the languid fire burn deep inside her, and knew that something would have to come to pass if she wanted to know what it was like to feel truly fulfilled. No matter how good kissing and safely exploring Hunter had been, it would not be enough tonight. She grabbed his hands and let her fingers curl around his. Sending some of the energy she was feeling through her touch, she let it tease his fingertips like static electricity.

He pulled her face up to meet his for a kiss. His lips were hot against hers. She did not even feel when the air started moving around her. When he moved his mouth away from hers, they were no longer standing outside the club. Lyssa looked around, carefully judging her surroundings. They were not at the Watch Tower, either. "Where are we?"

"Somewhere safe, away from our lives."

There were candles all around the room, and a king-size bed was in the middle. Its white satin covers contrasted deeply with the darkness of night. She could feel protective energy covering the room from all sides. No one would ever be able to detect them here, and no one would be able to enter. They were alone, and nothing from the outside world could distract them from what was about to happen. There was a faint warning in the back of her head, the one that always tried to surface whenever Hunter was close, but she shut it away this time. Those worries of a frightened young girl had no place in this woman's body. She was not afraid to feel any more. In fact, it was quite the opposite. It was like all the emotions that had been trapped tightly within her were ready to burst.

Hunter sensed a struggle within her and moved away for a moment, his back to her. "Lyssa, we don't—"

"Don't finish that." Lyssa reached out to touch his arm, and when he did not turn, she took a deep breath. "Please Hunter. Help me forget the world. Let me live in just this moment with you."

Lyssa heard the sadness in her plea, and Hunter heard it too. He turned around and put his hand on her face. She closed her eyes and let herself relax against it. It took only a second for the flames within her to respond to his nearness again. When she looked up at him, she saw the fires burning deep within his eyes too. When his mouth descended, she met him half way. Her fingers reached out to pull him closer to her, trapping themselves in his shirt. It disappeared quickly, and soon cloth was replaced with well-muscled flesh. She longed to feel his skin against hers.

"Ask and you shall receive," his hot breath whispered in her ear. She could not still the quiet whimper that responded to him. There was something to be said about having sweet nothings whispered in your ear. It made her all the more anxious for whatever came next.

While she concentrated on his breathing, she had almost not noticed that her shirt had been removed too. Hunter led her to the bed and they sank into it. She could feel the heat of his chest against hers. Lyssa ran her fingers down his back and arched against him when his lips seared a path down her throat. His guttural moan against her proved that he, too, was having trouble fighting back the invisible power that pulled them closer to each other. He reached behind her back to unclasp the bra that she was wearing, and his mouth moved down the valley of her breasts. Even though she did not move, her body jumped in ways she could not explain.

There was a sweet hot song running through their bodies, its melody much more delicious than either of them had anticipated. She let Hunter shepherd her to a place she had never visited before in this lifetime, as his hands and mouth seared her to the bone. They were both fully undressed, and their sweat soaked bodies were clinging to each other on the edge of something they could not explain. He paused for a moment, making sure that this was what she wanted.

"Please." Lyssa heard the plea leave her mouth in shaky breaths. There was something more here for them tonight. They could not leave it here. "Don't stop."

Hunter smiled down at her and left the bed for a moment. Lyssa realized at once that he was retrieving protection so that they could continue unhindered, and she made a mental note to look into other options for the future. She felt her chest flutter in anticipation, and then a slight apprehension for what might happen next nibbled at her composure. She shook the shadows of the past from her mind and reminded herself that this was her choice, that the love they shared far outweighed the shimmer of doubts within her.

"Are you still sure?"

Lyssa could sense the battle within him. It was clear that he wanted her to say yes, but tried to calm himself in case she said no. She knew he would not force the issue. She crawled to the side of the bed and pulled him to her. "I've never been more sure."

The tension left his body as he moved in beside her. The heat that had started to simmer rose once more. She was alive in the rise and fall of his breath, the beat of his heart so near to hers, and the strong arms that wrapped themselves around her. When they joined together, she felt complete. It did not take long for her to climb over the top. The world went almost black around her, as the wave of something entirely unexpected took her.

Hunter slowed down to let the world crash easily around her. He kissed her neck and ran his fingers down her body. She looked up at him questioningly, and he smiled secretively. "That was unworldly," she whispered to him. She sucked in a breath when he started to move within her again. Lyssa realized at once that he had not had taken care of his own needs yet as the desire rose between them again. This time, when she made it to the top of the world, he was right there with her, and when she jumped over the edge, he grabbed her hand and soared alongside her.

They stayed there together in the aftermath; their bodies glistened with sweat, and their skin glowed in the firelight. She ran her hand along his chest and breathed in the stillness that was surrounding them. They were both at peace with the world around them.

"Hunter?"

He looked down at her with eyes as heavy as hers. "Yes?"

"Let's not wait another lifetime to do this again."

He pulled her close and nuzzled her head with his nose. It was not making love that had made her feel complete tonight. It was the words longing to burst out of her mouth that did.

"I love you too, Lyssa," Hunter said to her quietly, before both of them closed their eyes to sleep.

Chapter 16

Lyssa did not need to open her eyes to know that she was alone in the bed. Hunter probably had to get up early today. But still, it would have been nice to wake up next to him. She moved her hands to where he had slept and was confused when her hands touched the icy cold sheets. When she opened her eyes, she saw that the candles had long simmered out. Hunter had been gone for quite some time. The lack of his face in the morning light made a pang of sadness enter her mind. Was he a morning person? Or was he a grump like her?

Lyssa looked around the floor for her things and found them easily. She dressed quickly and went to the mirror on the wall. Did she look changed? Should she? If anything, Lyssa felt different, a little more confident in her skin. Was this what a well-loved woman felt like? Lyssa would not let anything ruin this delicious feeling of contentment. She closed her eyes and pictured her room, and off she went.

It was clear that Hunter had stopped by her room, as there was a single red rose lying on the pillow of her bed. It was his way of apologizing for not being there in the morning. He had known she would come here next. She picked up the rose from the pillow and put it to her nose.

"Well, time for me to face the day." She showered and dressed for her morning before going down for breakfast with Jackson. As she sat down at the table, she made sure to put her thoughts on lock down. He did not need to read about what happened last night. That was private.

"Good morning," she greeted him, and was surprised to find Serena seated next to him.

"Happy belated birthday, Lyssa. I'm sorry that I missed it."

"Thank you, Serena. It was one of the best." Lyssa hoped that the smile she gave them did not betray her. She wished she could talk to Hunter today, but she knew he had gone back to his secret identity this morning and there was no guarantee when she would see him again. Lyssa hoped she would be too busy this week to miss his absence.

This week, Sector 4 was exploring more of the areas that Lyssa had catalogued and trying to cast out as many earth bound shadows as they could. They may not be able to annihilate many while they were in the Land of the Shadows, but they sure as hell would take out any they saw in their own world. Soon, they would start planning their attacks with other sectors, but until Julius felt that Sector 4 was more cohesive, he wanted them to stick together.

Since it was spring break, she spent that day tracking down more locations where the shadows had started gathering, then she marked it in the notes for the Watch Tower. Today, she was just finding them and passing on the locations. There would be no fieldwork. At least her work would give them a compilation of how many shadows were in each area, ultimately helping them track down the Craven.

Lyssa worked throughout the day and into the night. She was surprised that Hunter had not checked in with them yet, but she was afraid to voice her concern.

When he did not come home the next day either, she was very worried. Logan had not returned either. She finally could not stand the silence anymore. "Where are they, Julius?"

"With the Craven, I suppose. They'll return when they are able to. I wouldn't worry about it."

That sure was easy for him to say. If something happened to either one of them, Julius would easily replace them. Hunter was irreplaceable to her. She wanted to reach her energy to where he was, but would he feel it? Or would the Craven near him detect her presence if she attempted to locate him? Lyssa closed her eyes and tried to envision where he was. When she got close enough to almost find him, she felt her energy repelled. He was blocking her. He did not want her to see where he was or what he was doing, but he sent along a message to her. *I'm okay, Lyssa. I'll be home soon.*

Soon went from one day to a week, and then to several weeks. Lyssa knew that he and Logan were in deep, but her heart twisted inside her. She tried so hard not to worry about him, but part of her world was missing. Lyssa did not want to need him as much as she did, but it was too late for that. Jackson noticed her sadness and tried to comfort her.

"He'll be okay, Lyssa. He's coming home. You know he will," reassured Jackson.

"Do I? How can I know that? He's shut me out completely." Lyssa was about to add more to her tirade of emotions, but Julius entered the room.

"We can't wait much longer for them to return. We're going to attack them on their turf. First, we'll meet up with Sector 7. Gear up. Today we fight."

By gearing up, Julius meant grabbing their bag of magical items that they carried with them. Inside her bag, she kept the items that helped call her totem spirits, as well as her wand, crystals, and candles, in case she needed to cast a circle of protection. She took a minute to breathe in some calming air before joining the others in the library. She had never been to another area of the Watch Tower. How exactly would they get to Sector 7's area from there?

She was actually not surprised to see Julius open the hidden passage in the library again. This time, she noticed that he had pulled a completely separate book. When they walked through the door this time, there was no tunnel. Instead of the tunnel, they were staring directly at a brick building surrounded by several others. The building was run down compared to other buildings that she had seen in her lifetime. There was graffiti painted from one end to the other in red, blue, and black. A fire was burning in the trashcan outside it, but there was no one around to enjoy its flames.

They all climbed the stoop and entered the building. The carpet inside the old stairwell was so frayed that the wooden steps were visible beneath. When they reached the top, she realized they were on the seventh floor. Heaven help them if they had to meet up with Sector 30 in a building like this, for it seemed like they were in some inner-city ghetto. She followed Julius down the hall until he tapped on a door with the number seven stenciled on it. It swung open to let them in, and they walked inside.

Three guardians stared politely back at them. Lyssa listened as introductions were made, and bowed her head where appropriate in greeting. While she should be attending to what was being said, she could not help but worry about Hunter and Logan. She closed her eyes and tried to take in the moment.

The only man in the sector 7 was Jeremy. He had a low buzz cut and a face that looked haunted. He was wearing a white tank top and acid washed jeans. There were thick chains looping from the pockets at the front of his jeans, all the way to his large back pockets.

Sydney, a pale blonde with long wavy hair, was staring at her. She almost looked like a vampire with her deathly pale skin. She was dressed in a red short-sleeved shirt and dark blue jeans that hugged her hips.

The last one was a girl with long, straight, black hair. She wore a black v-cut shirt and black denim jeans, and black boots that went all the way up to her knees. The spiky heels were sharp and distracting. Her name was Ariel.

"Are there others?" If this was all there was to sector 7, it made her wonder if they would have enough fire power for their attack.

"We have others, but they are fighting another battle at the moment. Don't worry. We're up to the task."

"Of course," she added quickly. She should know better than anyone not to judge a book by its cover. "Forgive my curiosity. It sometimes gets the best of me."

"It does most of them," Ariel replied. She smiled softly at Lyssa and nodded her head at her.

"Lyssa, can you sense them?" Julius was already back to business.

Lyssa pulled out the map of her town and put it on the table in the middle of the room. She closed her eyes and ran her fingers over the map, trying to take in the energy source from the Craven. Her soul flew through the air to the warehouse she had been to before. As Lyssa peered in the windows, she saw that they were indeed inside. When one of them raised his head to the window, she looked him in the face. The shock overwhelmed her. It was Hunter. He quickly nodded to where her spirit was hiding, then quickly went back to what they were discussing. Lyssa noticed the black rings under his eyes, and his energy had been altered. She knew it was Hunter, but he was not the same as the last time she had seen him. Bringing her soul back to her body, she tried to hold in the gasp of shock that wanted to leave her body.

"Are they there?" Julius demanded.

Lyssa was not ready to answer the question yet. She needed time to understand what she had just seen. Lyssa attempted to shake off the bad feeling entering her body when she heard Hunter's plea. *You must come tonight. You must attack them. Don't let on that you recognize me when you're here. They need to believe that I am one of them.*

She pulled herself together and answered him. *We're on our way.*

"Yes, Julius. They're there. So are Hunter and Logan. We have to treat them as if we don't know them if we want them to get out of there safely."

"Agreed."

Lyssa pointed to the spot on the map. "We'll enter on the third floor and make our way up to the fifth."

A slight pop sounded, and Julius was the first to move through the air. The rest of them followed. When they entered the building, it was clear that they should move quietly. She kept replaying the image of Hunter in her mind. The hollowness of his expression sent chills down her spine. This assignment was sucking the life out of him.

The guardians climbed the stairs quietly, their wands out and ready. She was surprised to find no one was guarding the hallways. Were the Craven so confident in their abilities that they had no fear of intrusions? When they reached the doorway to the fifth floor, there was a rustle of movement behind the door. "*I think they heard us.*"

Julius turned around to face them. "*On three. 1, 2, 3.*" He kicked open the door and they rushed in behind him. Flash after flash of bright green light came shooting at them. They dodged each attack and countered with their own.

Jeremy pulled the chains from his pocket and started to wave them in the air. The chains started to gather energy with each swing, and soon were like electrically charged whips that he lashed around him. He was running at a Craven who had a rounded mole-like face, the man from her dreams. The Craven countered with his own blast of light, which was easily dodged.

Ariel was sending her totem animals at the Craven around the room. A spectral wolf was snarling at a woman it had trapped in the corner. She was in turn beating it with her wand, her fists, anything she could find, all to no avail.

Sydney called down an electric storm that shot sparks at any of the Craven in sight. Lyssa was impressed with their skills and wondered how long it had taken to master them.

Cement started to crumble as the room pitched around them. Clearly this building was too old to take the magical war waging within its walls. Lyssa sent bolt after bolt of light towards the shadows entering from the other end of the room. Various pieces of furniture made the perfect hiding places from ranged attacks, and the shadows all crouched behind them.

Lyssa saw Logan and Hunter amidst the fray. She knew there was turmoil within them. If they did not attack the guardians, their cover would be blown. She saw Hunter glance at her across the room, and he raised his wand. Lyssa knew he had to, and yet it made her sad to see him look at her with the dark sneer on his face. Gathering her senses, she guarded her facial expressions. Her head raised in challenge as she fired off her attack at the same time. She dodged his easily, but hers clipped him in the shoulder and knocked him to the ground. She fought the urge to run to him; instead, she hid behind the couch in front of her, taking in deep breaths to calm herself. Jackson put a hand on her shoulder to comfort her for one moment, then moved away and started attacking another Craven.

There was a loud rumbling, and the floors started to shake. When she looked up, she could see even more debris falling from the ceiling. The building was falling down around them, and if they were not fast enough, they would not be able to get out.

Lyssa was just about to teleport away when a pillar clipped her head mid movement. She tried to picture where she wanted to move to, but was having trouble concentrating. A hand pulled on hers, and she knew that someone else was moving with her. Lyssa knew who it was before they landed safely at the Watch Tower, where he placed her on the sofa quickly before leaving. When she tried to open her eyes, her head spun. Hunter had already left. She fell asleep thinking about the danger he was in, and hoping above all else that she had not hurt him with that blast she had sent at him.

Chapter 17

When she woke up in her bed later at her apartment, Lyssa felt empty inside. The only thing she wanted to feel was him. Closing her eyes, she pictured the one place where she felt closest to him. In moments, she was standing in their room. She lit the candles and crawled under the satin sheets, cradling his pillow next to her, trying to breathe in his scent. Did his spirit live here still? Could she feel him? No. The emptiness grew inside her, and the next thing she knew, she was sobbing into the pillow. She couldn't hold it back anymore. Her heart was breaking so far away from his. Did he feel the same emptiness? After a while, she fell asleep while the tears dried on the pillow.

It was even darker in the room when she awoke. The candles had almost burnt out. Now they were only small nubs with tiny spitting flames. Something had caught her attention while she was sleeping, but she could not figure out what it was. It was almost as if someone were calling out to her. *Lyssa?*

Hunter? Had she imagined it? She looked around the room, wishing he were there. When she did not get a response, she lay back down. It was pointless to go back to the Watch Tower tonight. She closed her eyes to go back to sleep, but then she thought she heard a slight whoosh of air enter the room. It was probably just her mind playing tricks on her. When she felt the hand on her face, she knew she was wrong. Lyssa opened her eyes cautiously.

"Lyssa. Sweet Lyssa."

She quickly threw the covers off and launched herself at him, almost tackling him in the process. She ran her hands over him to make sure this was her Hunter. Was he really there?

"Hunter. Are you okay?" Tears were forming in her eyes as she remembered attacking him earlier.

"I'm fine, Lyssa. No worse for the wear."

"But you are, Hunter. You look horrible. Are you eating? Have you been sleeping okay? Your eyes, they're haunted. What's happened to you?"

"Lyssa, I can't." It was clear that Hunter fought demons that he could not share with her. His soul was tortured with it. She longed to comfort him, but she had no idea what he needed.

"What can I do?"

"Help me feel."

Their lips easily sought each other in the darkness surrounding them. She put her hand to his face and felt the scratch of the hair that had started to grow. Gone was the clean shaven man that she had fallen for.

One soul-searching kiss led to many searing kisses that took her breath away. The fire between them was burning almost too quickly, and soon their clothing was holding them back. It disappeared within moments, and they lay there skin to skin. There was a desperation within her to hold on to him as long as she could. She wished she could capture this moment in time forever, lying so close with nothing separating the rhythm beating in their hearts.

Hunter rolled her onto her back and trailed kisses down her neck, the hair on his face scratching her neck in such an erotic way that she could not help the sudden arch of her back. When his teeth followed the same path in gentle nips, a low moan escaped her throat. He captured the next moan with his mouth, and she could feel the blood rushing to places that had been dormant in his absence. His hands roamed down her body as he continued to devour her lips. When he parted her legs with his hands and slid his finger between them, she almost lost her mind. Lyssa had to push his mouth away to take in a breath. She tried to push his hand away, because the feelings he was generating within her scared her. While she had let go before, this was something totally different, something wild and reckless.

"Relax, Lyssa," he whispered in her ear, and she almost lost control. "Let go," he said. He moved his hands in a way that made it hard for her to think. Her body tightened, and she braced for the impact as she crashed with wave after wave of tingling sensations running through her body. At her release, Hunter groaned and captured her bottom lip in his teeth. She could barely breathe; the world was spinning almost too quickly.

Her hands moved down his chest and felt his tight nipples under her thumbs. He sucked in his breath as her hands went lower. When she closed her hand around the length of him, he bucked against her. She could feel him pulse beneath her touch, and it made her heart race. Her head felt dizzy again as he moved against her hand. He ran kisses down her throat again, but did not stop until he reached a breast. Lyssa thought she would faint when he sucked on her nipple and massaged the other breast in his hand. Yes, this was dangerous. There was no hiding the emotions raging through their bodies. His other hand started massaging between her legs, and she was lost again. She could no longer tell up from down. The world was spinning, and all she could do was hang on to him.

The wave of passion overtook them. When he pulled away from her, she mourned his absence. He returned quickly, and she knew he was trying to be practical among this madness that coursed through them. When she expected him to enter her, she was almost disappointed, but when his hands started to stroke the fires between them again, she realized that she was rising even higher than before. She could barely catch her breath before the next wave hit, but the crash after that one took the rest of her reserve. Lyssa pushed against him, and he rolled to the bed. When she climbed on top of him and caught him between her legs, she felt his shaft pulsing. Lowering herself onto him, she caught her trembling bottom lip in her teeth and rode him until the world exploded around her. She fell forward, and he caught her with his hands. Both of them breathed erratically as she lay there on his chest. He stroked her hair and slid his other hand along her spine.

Lyssa rolled away and faced away from him. She was afraid to look at him. If she turned around and he was gone, she would be devastated. He rolled her back to him and took her face in his hands. Lyssa was unprepared for the gentle kiss he laid on her lips. Curling into him, she laid her face on his shoulder. It had only been a short time since she had last seen him, but she had missed him.

"I missed you too, Lyssa." It was as if Hunter had been surrounded by darkness, looking for a light to lead him home. They created their own light around them that burned far brighter than any candle ever could.

When she awoke in the morning, Hunter was still sleeping beside her. The easy rise and fall of his chest was comforting. She couldn't help the happiness beaming from every pore. He must have felt it, because he opened his eyes and looked at her.

"Good morning." He kissed her softly and pulled her close.

"You stayed," she whispered to him. "Do you have to go again?"

"Soon, but not yet." He pulled her close, and she suddenly remembered they had slept in the nude. When her skin moved against his, her heart beat loudly in her chest. Her breath caught in her throat when his hand ran down her spine. One kiss led to another, and they were caught up in each other again. Their bodies were dancing to a rhythm they could no longer ignore. When the song ended, they both started to fall back to sleep. Lyssa couldn't help but wonder what life would be if she could wake every day like this.

Elissa Daye

Chapter 18

When she woke up the second time, she was not surprised that Hunter was not there. He had stayed as long as he was able to, and she was more than willing to accept that. Lyssa rolled over and snuggled up to his pillow beside her. Images of their night together ran through her mind like footprints in the sand. The fires that burned between them would never be forgotten. She had never imagined that being intimate with another could leave her feeling so complete. As she closed her eyes, she could feel the satisfied smile turning up the corners of her mouth.

Letting out a yawn, she stretched her body. It was time to return to her duties. While she wished she could stay in this room forever, she knew she had to get back to the Watch Tower. They had to discuss their mission last night. She only hoped she was not going to be drilled for not remaining safely within its walls last night. It was not usual for a guardian to be away after a fight. They usually met briefly to check in with each other. While they may not be incredibly involved in each other's lives, they did care about the livelihood of their own.

After grabbing her clothes, Lyssa put on only essentials and carried the rest, as she was going directly back to her room at the apartment. When she teleported, she dropped her clothes in the hamper and looked around. Everything was as she had left it, but there was something different about it.

When she looked closer at her dresser, she saw a silver necklace sitting on top. It was a new locket, and when she opened it she could see Hunter's face looking back at her. A note was underneath it.

All you have to do is call.

She ran her finger over the locket one last time, then closed it carefully. Lyssa took off the old locket they had found before and pushed it under some socks in her top drawer. This was their past. They had a much different future.

She showered and dressed in new clothes for the day before heading into the kitchen. She knew she would have questions to answer. Jackson undoubtedly would have worried about her. When she did not find him in the kitchen, she knew he must be at the Watch Tower. Lyssa teleported into the parlor easily and found him sitting on the sofa. A knowing smile filled his face.

"You all right?" she asked him.

"Good. You?" By the way he kept his answer short, she knew he was a little peeved at her.

"I'm good. I'm sorry you worried. I would hate to say it won't happen again, but how long have you known me?"

"Exactly." Jackson stood up and walked past her with an impish smile on his face.

Lyssa followed him. When she turned the corner, she was surprised to find Hunter sitting in a chair in the hallway. Lyssa smiled at him and fought the urge to run to him. They had always tried to keep their personal lives separate from the other guardians. When she had almost walked past him, he reached out his hand and pulled her into his lap. She put her face in his shoulder and nuzzled his neck with her nose.

Apparently, he was no longer concerned with what the others thought. They stayed there for a few minutes, just enjoying the silence of their heartbeats. She broke away reluctantly when the number 4 on her arm started to light up. It was clear that they were being summoned together.

So many questions lingered between the light of the day, but she knew now was not the time. They would have much to say if they had time later. When they walked into the library together, she noticed the curious stares that she expected did not greet them. Serena smiled at her knowingly, and she could feel the heat rising up her face. She cleared her throat and offered a greeting, but almost stumbled over her words.

"It's okay, Lyssa. They know where you were last night."

"I'm sorry if you were worried."

"Hunter told us that he would find you. We thought it best that he see to you for the night." Was that a bit of discomfort in Julius's tone? When his eyes met hers, there was still concern etched inside them. He was worried about something, and because his mind was blocked, there was nothing she could do to decipher it.

Lyssa could only nod at him. What else could she say? While she was glad they were not asking her a lot of questions about where she had been that night, she still felt that Hunter should have told her that they knew where she was. There were a lot of things that Hunter should have told her last night, but those things would have to wait.

She sat down at the table and watched as the globe turned animatedly in front of them. A flash of yellow lights illuminated the map. The guardians all seemed to be accounted for at present.

The screen rolled down from the ceiling and instantly showed the bones of the demolished building. The news crew explained that a few bodies were being removed from the debris. Reporters were calling the victims inside some kind of miscreants that had taken up residence inside the abandoned building. The bridge leading to the building was closed off for the next few days so that the area could be made safe for anyone passing near it.

"We're all okay?" Lyssa could not help but ask, even though she could see that quite a few lights were showing for everyone to see. She did not like the sound of silence.

"Everyone is accounted for. There have not been any counterattacks on the Watch Tower. Chances are the Craven are still trying to figure out who attacked them last night. I'm hoping that Hunter can share some insight into their inner-workings."

Hunter nodded silently to Julius. He stood up and put his hand on the globe. The map of the town showed up immediately. "We have only successfully touched one branch of the Craven. They are all across their world. If you cut off one branch, others will swiftly emerge. They travel and thrive in groups of at least twelve. Last night resulted in five casualties. I've been dealing mostly with their local leader, The Mole. We are to be relocated until further notice and will be leaving this area. They are planning a major regrouping, but where, I do not know. I don't have as much useful information as I would like."

"It sounds like getting rid of the Craven will be the hardest part. Can we find out how to deactivate the portals they are opening? If we can at least slow down the emergence of the shadows, then perhaps we can remount an attack on the Craven."

"I agree, Julius. We need to focus on the shadows. If their numbers are allowed to grow too quickly, we will be faced with the new problems." Serena shook her head slowly, clearly thinking about what they had seen in the land underneath their feet.

"If they succeed in producing the new age of shadows we saw, it will be nearly impossible to fix the problem." Lyssa was still feeling her way into the discussion. She was trying not to let her mind wander. Something was pulling her away from the discussion. Closing her eyes, she started to listen to the silence around her.

Lyssa. There it was. She knew she had sensed something. Lyssa concentrated on the source, and when the others turned her way, she knew they had caught on to her dilemma.

"Lyssa? What is it?" Jackson looked over to her with concern etched in his hazel eyes.

"I'm being called. But I am having trouble hearing the voice. Someone is in danger. It's someone under duress. Just give me a minute." She shut them out of her thoughts quickly. *Who are you? Do I know you?*

Took you long enough. It's Lana. I'm trapped down here, and the shadows are coming. Please, you have to set me free.

Lyssa shook off a niggling suspicion that something was not quite right in this message. If it was Lana, then why did it not sound like the Lana she knew? "Something is all wrong. Somehow they have Lana, and are using her to get to me. But, it does not feel like it is actually Lana who is talking to me. How is that possible?"

"They have ways of making her talk," Hunter answered. His eyes started to glaze over, as if his memories had taken over his mind. He was also looking away, as if he knew something he could not share.

"What do we do?" Lyssa was worried about Lana, but she knew that as a Guardian of the Watch Tower, she had a duty to the entire world. If she ran and tried to save Lana, what would happen? She was sure it had to be a trap. How did she even know if she was still alive?

"There's not much we can do, Lyssa. If they have her, then she is already lost to you."

Lyssa slammed her fist into the table. It was devastating to hear what her mind already knew. Unfortunately, it was not easy to explain that to her heart. If the shadows had her, there was only one reason. Lana was dead. "Julius, please. You can't expect me not to look for her. Please let me look."

"Me too."

When he nodded at her, she closed her eyes and found her own quiet spot in her head to start the process of sending her soul to find Lana. She scanned all the places she would normally find her and was not surprised to find that she was not at any of them. Lyssa was drawn to the portal in the cemetery, and knew at once that Lana was no longer with the living. It was true; her soul had to be trapped in the Land of the Shadows.

She came back to her body instantly. When she looked up at the screen, she heard the report that they had identified the body of a student within the rubble. Someone had killed Lana and made it look like she was a casualty of the collapse.

"This has just gotten personal, you realize this?" There was a rage firing through her that scared even her. "How did they find her? You'll have to be much more careful, Hunter."

"I'm actually going in deeper now. The Craven have pulled both of us even closer into their folds since last night. I won't be able to check in with you until I find the information that we need. Logan and I will find a way to pass on the information, but we won't be able to leave the Craven for even a minute if we are to convince them that we're trustworthy. There's no other way." Hunter looked over to

Logan for agreement. When Logan nodded at Hunter, it was clear that they had made up their minds.

At this point, she knew it was the best thing for them to do, but it still made her heart heavy to know that Hunter was putting himself at a greater risk. If she was honest with herself, she knew he would have to return to them. Their job wasn't even half finished. Many things still needed to be accomplished to restore the proper balance to their world. The people of this world deserved a champion.

"What do we do in the mean time?" Serena looked to Julius.

"We continue to rid the world of more shadows. If we can't stop the Craven right now, perhaps we can at least continue to locate them. When we are able to learn the best method of attack, then we will know where to start."

"If we cannot remove a branch at a time, perhaps we need to learn how to remove the head. If we take out the hierarchy of the Craven, they will start to tumble." Lyssa looked over at Hunter. *We will talk before you leave*, her mind reached out to him. He nodded silently to her.

"Seems like we have a lot to prepare for. I will inform the others of what we have learned."

Lyssa bit off a sarcastic laugh and swallowed quickly. What they had learned was that the guardians needed to think before they acted. Innocent people could die if they ran off all half-assed like they did last night.

Looking back on it all gave her a bittersweet taste in her mouth. If she had been paying closer attention last night, would she have heard Lana reaching out to her? Would she have been able to save her? Her death rested on her shoulders, and it was the heaviest weight she would ever carry with her. A lot would change from here. She knew Hunter would be leaving, and she would not see him until they had better answers, but her heart felt colder. She could no longer focus her energy on him. Lyssa had to continue to fight the darkness climbing around them.

When they exited the room, Hunter grabbed her arm and made her face him. She did not want him to see the angry tears forming in her eyes. "Don't."

"Lyssa, it's not your—"

"Fault, Hunter? Yes, it is. If I had been looking out for my friends instead of myself, this would not have happened." She tried to remove her arm from his hands.

"That's it." Hunter pulled her closer, and they were suddenly flying through the air. All she could think was that she could not return to that room. She could not face the emotions rushing through her right now. Life had suddenly become much more complicated than she liked.

Lyssa did not care that they were standing in their favorite place. She pushed against him and tried to turn away. Hunter kept trying to pull her closer. She felt the energy within her rising higher, and her hair rose in the air around her. "Don't, Hunter. I swear you don't want to push me right now. I can't do this."

"Lyssa, you have to let it out. Don't hold it in. She was your friend. It's okay to mourn her."

"Mourn her?" she shrieked at him. "Mourn her? How can I do that, Hunter? When will I get that chance? I'm not sure I deserve to. I should have made sure she was safe. Where was she? You know they attacked her after we attacked them. How did they know?"

Hunter refused to look at her, as if he knew something that he was not telling her. She turned to him and pushed past the barrier in his mind. Something was terribly wrong. "Lyssa, Lana drew attention to herself. Her coven has been trying to track down the Craven. She got too close to them. That had nothing to do with you."

"Are you telling me that you knew about this?"

"I knew her coven was stepping over the limit, yes. I did not know they were going to attack her last night. I would have warned you, had I known."

It was too much to take in. Hunter knew that Lana could have been in trouble. Why did he not tell her? She sat down on the bench and tried to still the emotions raging through her. She knew that Hunter would not have let an innocent get hurt if he could have avoided it. She knew he would never wish any harm to those that she loved. These things she knew, but there was a part of Hunter that she no longer knew. It was a piece that had been bothering her ever since she saw him last night. Hunter was changing in ways she could not describe.

"You've changed, Hunter. The Hunter I fell in love with would have found a way to contact me."

"You're right. I should have contacted you. We could sit here and psychoanalyze the whole situation, Lyssa, but the only thing that remains true is that these Craven are destroying the world around them, one person at a time. From here on out, I will find a way to keep in touch with you; I have finally found a means of contacting you. It took me longer than I wanted, but I've found a way."

Lyssa still could not look at him. The anger was easy to show, an emotion with which she was quite familiar. There was no shame in the anger, but the tears that wanted to fall were painful ones. If they started, it would be hard to make them stop. Lana was such a courageous young witch. Her friend could have had such a life ahead of her, and now what did she have? Her bright light was snuffed out before it even got to shine. Her soul wasn't even free to rest.

When she thought she had fought back the misery within, the tears started to fall. Lyssa could hold them back no more than a broken levy could hold a swelling river. She did not fight Hunter's embrace when he lent his healing energy. The tears were soon followed by sobs that robbed the very breath from her chest. They sat there for what felt like an eternity as she mourned her friend, but she mourned much more than her dear departed friend. She cried for the happiness she had started to feel with Hunter, knowing that the beauty that had been them was now completely scarred by tragedy. Lyssa should have known that happiness always came with a price.

When she finally caught her breath and could look at Hunter without tears blurring her vision, she came back to the last thing he'd said to her. "How will you keep in touch Hunter? Please don't put yourself at risk for me. I couldn't bear it if I lost you, too."

"Your necklace. Wear it at all times, and you will be able to find me. As long as you wear it or keep it near, I can find you. Our thoughts will travel to each other, as long as our minds are open. You will not be able to reach me at all times, but I will be able to reach you."

"Will they be able to find the link between us?" Being able to reach him when she needed him was nice, but not if it came with a price.

"No. They will not. I have been working to block anything that I do not want the Craven to find. They will never find you, Lyssa. You and the Watch Tower are safe. Only the guardians will have enough weapons to attack the Craven. We just have to find their weakness first."

"Yes. No more half-assed plans. I'll make sure we wait for whatever information you can provide." Lyssa looked away from him. Yes, this was easier. If she continued to keep this conversation more business and less personal, maybe her heart would sting less when he left.

"Lyssa."

Great, he knew she was deflecting again. Lyssa looked at him with a raised eyebrow. "What?" she asked defensively.

"I'll be home as soon as I can. I'm still here for you. Please don't shut me out."

"What do you want me to say, Hunter? My heart was breaking every second you were away, and I'm about to face the same thing, only this time I fear you may not come back."

"I'll always come back." He kissed her tenderly, and while she should have been appeased by the sentiment, the thoughts swirling in the back of her head prevented her from just letting go. Yes, he might come back, but he would never be the same. He was fooling himself if he thought differently.

They traveled back to the Watch Tower before he left again. This time her world felt a little colder and darker than before. She would put every effort into finding ways to bring down the Craven as quickly as possible. She had her whole world to save, and he was growing into a stranger more and more each day.

Elissa Daye

Chapter 19

From the moment Hunter left, she pushed herself into her work. Her schoolwork suffered a bit, but she maintained a passing grade in all her classes. Jackson tried to get her more involved with the real world around her, but she refused to listen. She spent every waking hour staring at the globe in the library trying to locate the Craven's latest movements. She had located a few, but it seemed every time she got closer to them, they moved further away. Hunter had said that they could not detect her, but she disagreed. If she was not careful, they would find her. From time to time, she took a break from tracking their movements and started locating the actual portals that led to the Land of the Shadows. There were many souls trapped in the lands below, and one of them was Lana. Lyssa would find a way to set her free, if it was the last thing she did.

Lyssa desperately wanted to keep Jackson out of the line of fire too, but he was as furious with the Craven as she was. While he wanted revenge, he also understood that there was danger in retaliation. Even so, neither one of them would rest until Lana's death was avenged. He spent his time researching through the ancient texts in the library, hoping to find a way to bring Lana back. It was a desperate attempt to achieve the impossible. There was no way to bring her physically back to this world. Her body was no longer with the living, and who knew what had happened to her soul.

Lyssa had stood by his side when her coffin was lowered into the ground while cold tears streamed down her face. Before she knew it, angry sobs left her and she lost all control. Jackson had put his arm around her, and they commiserated together. People were staring at her as if she had lost her mind. They all had stood so stoically around the grave, but Lyssa could not contain the sadness she felt for the loss of such a wonderful light. She had lost many people in her life, but not the ones who truly mattered. Lana had been so much more than a friend to her. Her first year of college would have been miserable had they not met. She remembered how often she had eaten alone the first few weeks of school, wishing that she had someone there to talk to. While Lyssa had found her freedom from her past in college, she had also discovered a great loneliness. In an attempt to make a new path for herself, she had approached Lana as they both walked to the cafeteria and asked the blonde if she would mind company. Lana had flinched at first, as if Lyssa were some weirdo ready to pounce on her, but after a second's hesitation, Lana shrugged her shoulders and welcomed her along. It had been a fast friendship, and life had suddenly become less lonely. It had only improved along the years when Jackson transferred to her school as well.

Lyssa tried to shake away the sadness that entered her mind every time she remembered her dear friend. It was time to focus on the task at hand and ignore the guilt that ate at her soul. She could only do so much to save her world, and she could not save everyone…even Lana had known that. If Lana were here now, she would tell her to continue to fight the shadows. What bothered her most was that even with all these powers, she was limited. Did the Craven feel limited in any way? Did shadows have limitations? From what she could see, they were learning how to overcome anything that seemed to hold them back. Lyssa was starting to feel like she had not put enough time or effort forth, and even the bags growing under her eyes would not stop her from pushing through. They had all been feeling less than rested.

Days turned into weeks, weeks into months, until she had been there with the Watch Tower for almost a year. She had not seen or heard from Hunter since he had left, and he had given them very little information on his mission as of late. Hunter had to block her to protect his mission, so she rarely pushed her thoughts forward to find him. She missed him, but she had to put those feelings aside. Even though she hardly acknowledged his existence, she still wore the locket that he gave her...a part of her still needed to have a connection to him. Lyssa could sense him, so she knew he was all right, but her heart was heavy any time she thought of him, so she constantly had to push him to the back of her mind.

Jackson had told her to write him off and move on, that she deserved to find happiness somewhere else, but Lyssa just could not let go of her feelings for him. Not like she had much time to dwell on it, with trying to track down Lana's soul and finding a way to deal with the shadows. Whatever she had felt or needed no longer seemed to matter. One day bled right into the next, and at times she did not know which way was up.

She had been tracking and recording for such a long time that she was wearing herself to the bone, and Julius had finally felt the need to intervene. "Lyssa. Enough. You're no good to us if you're exhausted."

Lyssa looked up at him with eyes that ached from too much concentration. He was right. She needed to get away from this for a moment. "Fine. What else can I do?"

"Come with me." He reached out his hand, and she took it trustingly. He may have done some brash things, but she trusted him.

When she opened her eyes, she was surprised to find herself in the cemetery they had visited before. Why were they back here? She looked up at Julius, trying to understand why he would have brought her here. "Julius?"

"We're going to take a stroll."

"In a cemetery? Really?" Lyssa bristled at the easy sarcasm that entered her voice. Did she really have to be at odds with everyone around her?

Julius walked her to a different area of the cemetery. There were several smaller tombstones with very little lettering on them. She could see a few names on a handful of them, while others were blank with just a date of death. No one had been able to identify the people buried beneath. The only things they had in common were that they had died in this city, and all the dates of death fell within the past two years. There were close to twenty lost souls beneath her. Their souls were probably trapped underground too.

"Okay. So what exactly are you trying to tell me here, Julius?" Lyssa eyed him warily.

"We have all lost someone, Lyssa. We all know how you're feeling. Every soul here had someone who loved them. We cannot take back the pain. We cannot erase the loss. We can do what they have always done."

"And what is that?"

"Live to fight another day."

"What? That's it. Here you are standing in front of these graves, and you want to spout that crap to me? If you knew someone here, it wouldn't be so easy for you to stand here and say we've done everything we could. There is always something more we could have done."

"My little sister is buried here. She was only sixteen when the shadows drove her into taking her own life. I want nothing more than to spend every minute of my life searching for her lost soul in the Land of the Shadows, but I have to remember all the people who are with the living first."

"Their souls should not be any less important than the living. They cannot live again if they are shackled to this lifetime. I've had enough waiting, Julius. I want to start searching the Land of the Shadows. There just isn't enough information available about it. I want to enter other portals and find what is powering these damn shadows. Every entity in this world is fueled by some kind of energy. Evolution has changed them so that they can feed on the energy of others, but where do they begin before all this occurs?"

Julius looked at her speculatively before answering her. "I had a feeling you would say that. I agree that we need to do more research about the Land of the Shadows. The Craven are getting a lot of their powers through the darkness they are channeling through the shadows. They are both parasites feeding off each other in some kind of symbiotic relationship. If we can stop the rising of the shadows underneath us, then the Craven could be defeated. They are like psychic vampires draining the life from others wherever they can."

"Why are we talking about this here, Julius? Why not in front of the others?"

"Because this is not something mandated by the Watch Tower. It would be incognito, and you would be on your own."

"You would send me in on my own? Without Jackson?"

"Let's be honest for a minute. You and I both know that I couldn't stop you. Look, Lyssa, I know what road you are meant to travel. I've already seen it. You are destined to unravel the mystery in the Land of the Shadows while we fight them here. Hunter and Logan are learning more about the Craven each day so that we can find a way to break the cycle of energy between them. But you, Lyssa, you are meant to find the key to it all. Jackson has his own niche as a guardian, but you both have separate destinies."

"Wow, that's a tall order." Lyssa took a deep breath. That was a lot to put on one person, a lot to take in one afternoon, but he was right. She would not stop until she found a way to save the souls trapped underground, and to do that she had to know what made the shadows tick. Lyssa had a lot more work to do than she first thought, and he was right about Jackson. He had another path within the Watch Tower.

"You'll still have responsibilities at the Watch Tower. Otherwise, the others will wonder what you're up to. I trust you'll be careful when you go."

"You can count on it. I've already located some portals that I would like to investigate."

"Get some rest first."

"You got it."

Chapter 20

Lyssa returned to the Watch Tower and pretended that the conversation with Julius had never happened. No one else needed to know what they had discussed. Julius was right. Sometimes they had to take things into their own hands. She now had a little more respect for him as a leader. He knew that they could not always be at a standstill with the world. Sometimes they actually had to act, even when others thought it was easier to wait for answers.

During the next day, she researched and cataloged information just like every day before, but the way that she looked at the world had changed. She had been feeling held back and helpless. Now Lyssa felt empowered and encouraged. If anyone could find the answers to the origins of the shadows, it would be her. It was not like she had much else to look forward to right now. Hunter had disappeared from her life so easily, and while she should be able to contact him, she had not been able to for some time. Being able to only barely sense him made her feel completely disconnected, and she started to feel a wall building up around her. Lyssa could not focus on how she felt about him right now. If she dwelt in the bitterness of their separation, she would not be of any help to anyone else.

Her appetite had returned, and she was suddenly hungry for a good dinner. She ignored the stares from the table when she devoured the food that Jackson had prepared. He always made extra whenever Serena came, in hopes that Lyssa would sit down and eat for a change, and today was a good day to start. Lyssa thought about all the work she had ahead of her and smirked. She couldn't help wondering if she had bitten off more than she could chew.

"So what gives?"

"Hmm?" Lyssa concentrated on washing the cup she was holding.

"Why so chipper?"

"Well, I can either dwell on things I cannot change, or I can work on changing the things that are within my realm of possibilities."

"Have you heard from Hunter? Is that what happened today?"

"Nope. Not that it would change things if I had, Jackson. We can't be together right now. We may have had something while he was here, but we are definitely on break now that he is gone." Lyssa pursed her lips at that comment. Is that how she truly felt about Hunter right now? Did she still love him? People always said that absence makes the heart grow fonder, but whoever first said that was a certifiable idiot. She was not fond of Hunter right now. She was downright pissed at him. It was not like she didn't know that he had to be where he was, but why even bother making her fall for him if he were just going to drop off the face of the planet?

"You can't mean that, Lyssa. I know how much he means to you." Serena was looking at her sadly.

Lyssa laughed out loud. "Really? I am doing the healthiest thing I could be doing right now. I'm moving on and focusing on what I really need to work on. Come now, Serena, you must recall the embittered, self-conscious person you met when I first walked in that door. Do you want me to be the same simpering idiot who pines after someone she can't have?"

"But you have him, Lyssa. He'll be back. Sooner than you think."

"I'm not holding my breath, Serena. Look what happens to the people I love. I'd do better to focus on our mission to rid the world of the shadows. Please, just drop it. I'm okay. I'm doing me right now, that's it. M-E."

"Sing it sister!" Jackson smiled and gave a sassy swish of his head.

"As long as you're okay."

Serena did not seem happy with any of her responses, but she did not know her agenda. If she was able to solve some of the puzzles of the Land of the Shadows and how they were being created, then she might actually be able to bring Hunter home before any more damage was done to his soul. For now, she would not be sitting around waiting for him to contact her. As she told Serena, she was going to do what she needed to do, just as Hunter was.

When everyone had finished for the evening, she yawned and made it clear that she was heading up to her room for the night. Since the only person who had ever disturbed her in her room was Hunter, it was pretty easy to assume she would be left to her own devices. Lyssa had already found at least six portals that she would like to enter, but tonight she was revisiting the first portal she had entered to see if there was any more information to be found. She looked through her closet to find clothes that would allow her to camouflage herself. If she looked like one of the shadows below, maybe it would be harder to be detected. Lyssa found a black pair of jeans, black boots, and a black hooded sweatshirt. A black mask would complete the whole look perfectly, but she did not have one, so covering her head with the hood of the sweatshirt would have to do.

Lyssa closed her eyes and pictured the cemetery she had visited before. Instead of moving to the entrance of the cemetery, this time she teleported to the tree beside the portal. She hid there in the darkness for a few moments to make sure that no one was watching her. The night was quiet like any other, and the graves cast shadows on the ground from the moonlit glow above. When she was sure the cemetery was empty, she stepped out from behind the tree and moved near the portal. She felt the space in front of her get colder when the vortex of the portal was giving off frigid air. This time she mentally prepared herself for the pitch black of the cave inside as she stepped through the portal.

Her eyes slowly adjusted, and she started to move cautiously through the darkness in front of her. When she had made it to the stairs of the subway, she looked above carefully. It was no darker here than it was before, even though it was the still of night in her world above it. A cool breeze floated across her face, and she saw newspapers scatter across the ground like tumbleweeds. Shadows were in the far distance, but she was not troubled by their appearance. They were headed away from her, and from what she could see, they looked much like her, all in black from head to toe. She pulled out her wand and used it to make her aura mimic the air around her. She felt the air swirl around her and coat her like a blanket. If this worked correctly, it would be the best cloaking device ever invented. The only true test would be to get closer to a shadow and see if they noticed her. If they did, she would have to teleport out of there quickly. While she was tempted to find this out right away, she knew that was only part of her mission tonight.

Tonight she wanted to speak with other lost souls to see if they had any information that would help her free them.

Lyssa went to the building across the street as she had before. When she climbed the stairs and opened the door, she was saddened to realize that the souls that had been there before were no longer present. Instead, charred marks now stained the floor like pools of black blood.

She walked over to the stains and put her hand over them. Her mind soaked an imprint from them as flashes of pictures entered her head. Lyssa saw the shadows enter the room, then the blast of fiery light from blackened fingertips that seared each soul. Their screeching cries echoed horribly around her. She had always thought that pain ended when you died, but it was very clear from the impressions on the floor that there was still pain after death if the soul was not allowed to ascend to its final resting place. The rest of their life's essence pooled on the ground like crude oil as the imprint continued. Moments after their souls had been obliterated, the puddles boiled over, and a black smoke rose from the puddles. It rose higher and wafted towards the shadows standing near the door. The shadows raised black crystals towards the smoke that acted like quiet vacuums, sucking what was left of the souls and trapping them firmly inside. She raised her hand away from the floor and felt herself shiver as she tried to wave away the evil vision she had just seen. If this was what happened to Lana, there would be hell to pay.

Was that how the shadows were getting the energy to expand their abilities? Wasn't it bad enough that these things were corrupting the innocent thoughts of others to the point that death seemed a much more pleasant alternative than living their lives? Now these shadows were feeding and growing from the souls they had trapped beneath the surface.

This was bad. This was so much worse than they had imagined. But this by itself was not enough information for the Watch Tower. She did not have conclusive proof that these beings were formed completely by devouring the souls of others. There was still much more research to do.

Lyssa decided to continue her exploration of this area and find out if the shadows could detect her within their radius. Walking down the stairs, she entered the street carefully. From what she remembered, the shadows had been moving down this street away from where she had started, so Lyssa decided to keep going to where she had last seen them. As she walked down the street, she looked at the buildings surrounding her. There was no energy soaking through the walls, nor any spirits screaming for release. It was like a deserted city. She couldn't help but wonder if their last excursion here had made the shadows wipe the souls out of existence. Lyssa would have to be very careful not to leave any trail of her energy in this world.

Lyssa searched for hours before she actually found another shadow walking about. Could it be that the shadows were not present in the witching hours? Would this be the time they spent stalking the innocents in the human world? If that was the case, wouldn't this time of night be the best time to help the souls trapped here? It was a hypothesis that would need further research.

Lyssa crept closer to the shadow to test her shield and was happy to find it did not turn as she got closer. When she got near enough to almost touch it, the shadow stopped. She ducked into the stoop of a doorway to her left. Standing there quietly, she kept as flush to the door as possible, her head looking down to the ground, so that her hood would conceal her head while holding her breath. The shadow turned toward her, but then it turned back around and started to move forward through the empty street. Lyssa let a breath out slowly and inhaled another just as quietly. So the shadow could sense her if she got too close to it, but when there was enough distance between them, she was safe enough. These were all interesting details she would need to report to Julius when she had enough information to act.

When it was safe again, she followed behind the shadow at a farther distance, so as not to be detected. The shadow was soon joined by two others. None of them turned around to look at her. When she had been tracking them for close to an hour, they neared another subway terminal and started to climb into its depths. Part of her felt extremely leery about following them into a dark tunnel. They would have the advantage, as she would not be able to see nearly as well as they could, but she knew there had to be something down there that drew them to it.

Ever so slowly, she entered the tunnel behind them. Lyssa had her wand stashed up her sleeve in case she needed to use it to defend herself, but it seemed unnecessary. These beings were being pulled to something she could not feel. It was almost as if a large magnetic force was drawing them closer. She mimicked their movements and moved closer to the entrance to another tunnel.

When she looked inside the entrance, Lyssa saw something that almost turned her stomach. The shadows had all gathered around a large black sphere that appeared to be made of some kind of obsidian stone. They raised their wands, and a swarm of black dots flew towards the orb like locusts, some kind of dark energy. She recognized the energy at once. It was the same helpless feeling that she had felt when the shadows were feeding on her soul. It was the same oily substance as the black pools staining the floors in the building. This was what they were doing with the energy from the stolen souls.

Lyssa stepped through the entrance and moved to the side of the closest wall. She stood there, transfixed with their ritual and breathless with a silent rage building inside her, and yet she had to stay there. A need to find out as much as she could consumed her. As she watched the ritual reach completion, another clue presented itself. The stone pulsed like a charcoal heart, rising and falling, and a staccato beat sounded around the tunnel. Before her eyes, a blob of darkness started to pulse from one side of the orb. It grew in shape and form, so large that it was like a child ripping itself from its womb. She was awestruck with what she was seeing…the birth of evil so slow and simple. Three more shadows formed from the orb and grew to standing size. Clearly, these rocks were responsible for the continued growth in the shadow population, being fed with the energy that these leeches sucked out of the helpless people of her world. Lyssa wanted to attack it, but she knew that being hotheaded would not lend itself to her research. She had to get out of there while she still could. The shadows kept pooling forth from the orb, and it was clear that if they kept multiplying within this tunnel, she would be detected. Lyssa exited the tunnel and teleported directly home.

Chapter 21

When she went to the library the next day, Julius was there waiting for her. "I need to talk to you, Julius."

"So talk."

"Without interruption."

"I see. The others are out for the moment, but I'll make this an eavesdropping free room." He pushed a button and all the doors shut, and the click of a lock assured her that no one would enter. When a yellow energy shield started to run across the sides of the room and burned into the floors and ceilings, she knew that they would be uninterrupted from teleportation as well.

"Better?"

"Yes. Last night I revisited the first portal that we went into. I found a few valuable things. First, I learned that it is possible to use stealth in the Land of the Shadows to prevent detection. It was easy to camouflage myself in black to look just like one of their own. I knew this would not be enough by itself, so I used some magic to create a cloud of the black energy swirling around me."

"Were you able to get close to the shadows?"

"The cloaking works up until about six feet away. When you get closer than that your own energy starts to be detected."

"This is good. We can start exploring the portals more clearly from here. What else?"

"The souls that are trapped down there are in great peril, Julius. They are using some kind of dark magic to incinerate the souls into pools of energy that they are feeding on. We have to free them, Julius, not only because it is the right and just thing to do, but also because this energy is being used to create more shadows."

"Did you see this with your own eyes?"

"I knew you were going to ask me that. I followed them down into another tunnel that branched into even more tunnels. They had crystals that trapped the siphoned souls into them, and were using them to send the energy to these orbs that seem to act as a power station for the shadows. Not only is it powering the ones that are already in existence, it is manufacturing more, many more."

Julius pursed his lips thoughtfully. "This is all useful information."

"So now what, Julius?"

"We need more information, Lyssa. I can't take this to the Watch Tower elders if I don't have enough supporting information. You'll have to enter more portals."

"Julius?"

"Yes?"

"What have you heard from Hunter? Have you heard anything from Logan?"

He looked uncomfortable in his chair, and she knew he must be keeping something from her. "I know what I've already shared with everyone else."

"You're deflecting, Julius. I've known you long enough to know when you are hiding something."

"All I can tell you is that he is deep undercover, Lyssa. The Mole has given him entrance to the leaders that will move him up the branch in the Craven."

Lyssa could tell he was trying to protect her from something; what that was, she was unsure of, but she knew that she would not rest until she had found out for herself.

When they had finished the conversation, she teleported directly to her room. Lyssa sat on her bed and thought over her options. She could continue to wait and hope that Hunter would return, or she could use the same cloaking method and search him out. Sit and wait forever, or take action? The reasonable part of herself told her that their mission was more important than any of their personal lives, but the injured heart in her chest beat out its own pleas, especially if she could see his face for even a moment. Would she still feel the excitement she had felt when she first fell for him? There was only one way to find out.

Lyssa opened up a map of the U.S. and set her mind to locating him. She put one hand on her locket and tried to lock on to his energy. When she felt it, she put her hand on the map. Letting it fall over the different states, she stopped only when she felt a pulse of energy leap into her fingertips, for she knew that she had found him. She closed her eyes and made the leap through space to where he was.

It was a dark, crowded nightclub, and the music was pumping loudly. The room was filled with hot bodies dancing within strobe lights that beat out a fantastic lightning rhythm. She could see a few Craven close to her that were walking upstairs, and quickly she looked down. For good measure, she put her hand around the wand in the long front pocket of her hooded sweatshirt and recast the cloaking. Lyssa climbed the steps cautiously, avoiding any eye contact with people around her.

When she reached the top of the stairs, her heart almost leaped out of her chest. There he was, safe and sound. The joy was soon replaced with aching horror. He was not alone. A woman leaned over the booth behind him and pulled his face around for a kiss that lasted almost a lifetime. When he reached around and pulled her into his lap, she sucked in her breath. He was no longer her Hunter. He was someone completely different, and the shock froze her heart like dry ice and threw it to the ground to shatter into a million jagged pieces. No wonder Julius avoided her questions.

Hunter? Would he hear the pain in her thoughts? Would he even pull himself up for air long enough to have heard it? Lyssa watched as his face turned thoughtful for a moment, but when he didn't respond to her plea for him, she walked closer to his booth. She thought even with her energy masked he would feel her. He looked up for a moment, but she turned her back quickly on him.

Lyssa almost tripped as she ran down the stairs and waded through the bodies waving wildly around her. It would have been better had she not seen him there. The logical part of her tried to remind herself that Hunter was undercover. He had to convince the Craven that he was one with their sect. She tried so hard to remember this, but the tears were already starting to climb down her face when she left the building. Lyssa clenched her hands at her side and desperately attempted to still the flurry of emotions running through her. She kept walking, not caring where her destination was, just wanting to get rid of the pain, wanting to feel the numbness that she had created around herself before Hunter had thawed her out. The fool who said it was better to have loved and lost then never to have loved at all clearly had never felt the pain of losing someone so cruelly.

Lyssa sat down on a bench near a bus stop and waited for the bus to come, for she was not ready to return home. When it arrived, she walked stoically up the steps and paid her fare. She rode the bus for hours, well into the morning, as the dawning light streamed through the windowpanes. The bus driver had not questioned her as the tears flowed silently down her face through each stop. She stayed there, slumped over in the seat, unable to move, to do anything but simply feel the hurricane of emotions running through her.

Lyssa didn't notice when someone sat down opposite her. She never looked up. And when a voice entered her solitude, she almost did not recognize it. "Lyssa, please." There was desperation in the voice reaching out to her.

Shaking her head from side to side, Lyssa couldn't answer him. What could she possibly have left to say to him? She never looked up at him, not even when she rose from her seat and exited the bus. She was about to turn the corner when his hand touched her shoulder. He tried to get her to face him, but she just could not.

"Please, just look at me."

Lyssa took a deep breath, steeled her confidence, and turned around to meet his gaze. "Did you need something?"

"For you to understand."

"What is there to understand, Hunter? You're on a mission, and you have a cover to keep. End of story." She started to move away from him and was about to teleport away when he called her again. There was an aching sadness in his voice.

"Please, Lyssa, you're the only light I have left."

"I was the only light that you had left, Hunter. I don't feel like any kind of light right now. You do what you have to do. The Watch Tower needs you. I don't." Lyssa took off the necklace he had given her and dropped it in his hands. Taking a deep breath, she returned to her room before she could change her mind. She could feel the sorrow in him before she left, but it was a party compared to the feelings that ran through her own heart.

Elissa Daye

Chapter 22

Lyssa wanted nothing more than to separate herself from Hunter right now. So much time had been spent waiting for him to come home, and it was nothing but wasted energy. She kept seeing his face from the last time she saw him, shadowed and slightly frail. Lyssa prayed that the Craven did not take his very essence away from him. She may still be reeling in pain, but she wanted nothing but the best for him.

Lyssa was deep in thought in the parlor at the Watch Tower when she felt a hand on her shoulder. She jumped up and almost screamed her head off until she saw Hunter standing by her. "What are you doing here, Hunter?"

"I had to make sure you were okay."

Lyssa closed her eyes and tried to gather her wits. She let out a long compressed sigh. "You didn't need to come. I'm fine. Go back to your mission." She sat back down on the couch and curled up under the afghan, her body now facing the wall.

"You're mad at me. I don't blame you. You must think the worst of me right now."

Lyssa didn't just hear the sadness in his voice. She felt it call out to her like an echo across a void. It chipped through the barrier of ice she had started to grow around her, but she kept trying to deflect it. Lyssa refused to turn around. She thought for an instant that he had left, and panic hit her heart like a jackhammer. She sat up and turned back around to see him standing by the window, his back turned, facing desolately away from her. A tear formed in her eye.

"What do you want?" Her throat was threatening to close on her.

He turned around and looked at her in a way that broke her heart. She looked at him closely. His hair was disheveled, and while he had shaved his face recently, he looked haggard. He had not been eating properly. He was dressed in black from his head to his toes. The light that had once surrounded him was being blocked by the night.

"You've changed too, Lyssa. You're stronger. I wish you could see the woman I see." Lyssa half expected to see him smile, but it was as if the man she was looking at no longer knew how. Was his heart hurting as much as hers? Did she even realize the sacrifice that he was making for them all? She'd been so wrapped up in herself that she had not thought about how he must be feeling.

Lyssa put her hand on his shoulder, and a flash of light entered her mind. In an instant, that flash was replaced with an image of an older Hunter smiling down at a young boy, whom she could only assume was Hunter's by the pure joy reflected on his face. The Hunter she knew was still in there somewhere. He still had a bright future ahead of him. She suddenly knew that he was going to make it out of this ordeal just fine. When she saw a woman walk onto the porch behind him, she could not believe her eyes. When she moved her hand off his shoulder, Hunter looked deep into her eyes. "You saw it, didn't you?"

"Saw what?" Lyssa tried to dodge the question.

"Please tell me what you saw."

Lyssa looked away from him. She did not want to share what she'd just seen. She didn't believe it to be real, not after what she'd seen last night. She couldn't bear to think of it. "No."

"Why not, Lyssa?"

"Because what we want no longer matters."

"It doesn't have to be that way." A hint of desperation entered his voice.

"Yes. It does."

Hunter closed the distance between them and tried to cradle her in his arms, but she pushed him away. She wanted more than anything to fall into him, but she could not give in. She had been holding it together the best that she could these past few hours, hours that had quickly felt like eternity. Lyssa could not help the tears that ran down her cheek. Was it selfish to want someone so much that you wanted to forget the rest of the world? Yes. Of course it was. It always was, and that was why she had been desperate not to fall for him.

"Hunter?"

"Yes, my love?"

Lyssa had never heard him call her that before, and it rattled her nerves even further. He was not giving up. "When are you coming back?" Lyssa felt childish for asking for something she knew she could not have, like a child pining for the last cookie in the cookie jar. She knew they had to uphold the peace, love, balance, and life of others, but how were they supposed to do that successfully when they were constantly reminded that those things were missing from their own lives?

"I can't answer that right now."

She nodded without a sound. Lyssa had already known the answer. He had to go back. He would always go back. His mission would always come first. That was really the way it should be. She rallied up the defenses that she had been using to get through his absence and pushed away from him. "I shouldn't have asked that. I know you're doing what is best for the world."

This time she was the one looking out the window trying to gather her composure. She looked down at her feet and squeezed her eyes shut, hoping to stuff the tears back into her eye sockets. Where was the anger? It was safer to deal with, much easier to mold into a plan of action. There was no plan here, just an emptiness that she knew would grow into a gaping, festering wound that there would never be a cure for. It was time to focus her energy on the Land of the Shadows and try to find Lana. Her attempts to learn more about the shadows would help distract her from the mess between them. "You should go."

"Don't send me away like this," Hunter pleaded with her.

"Like what, Hunter? You have a mission to do. So do I. It's all that really matters." Lyssa walked to the door and started to turn the handle, but she just couldn't do it. She needed him to free her, but ached for him to hold her near.

"It won't be forever, Lyssa," he tried to soothe her.

"It already has been, Hunter. Don't worry. I've survived much worse than this. I'll survive you too." Lyssa could see the tears forming in his eyes, but the cold-hearted bitch she was channeling could not resist. "Goodbye, Hunter."

Since he would not leave, she teleported away from him. She used her cloaking spell to hide from the world and quickly set up shields that would keep him from teleporting into their apartment. Lyssa knocked on a door and almost crumbled into Jackson's arms when he opened the door to his room. He held her there for moments before he helped her move inside.

"Oh honey!" He motioned to his friend Adam, and they both helped move her to the couch in the living room.

The Land of the Shadows

Lyssa spent the next three days recuperating with Jackson at her side. When Julius had come to find her, Jackson had shooed him away. When Serena came looking for her, he chased her off. When Hunter tried to come see her, Jackson slammed the door in his face. After she had cried as much as a grieving person could cry, she decided it was time to get back to work. People were counting on her.

When she returned to the Watch Tower, Julius was surprised to see her. He nodded to her quietly and gestured to the seat next to him. "Sit."

"Julius, I...,"

"No explanation needed, Lyssa. I'm just glad to have you back. I almost thought...."

"That I was not coming back? This job is bigger than me, Julius. I just needed some time and space to get my thoughts in order. I'm ready to get back to work."

"Hunter is back with the Craven for the time being. He's moving up higher in the ranks."

"I don't need an update anymore, Julius. I've closed that chapter in my life."

"Lyssa, you should know that he asks about you every day."

"And how exactly does that information help me focus on my mission at hand?" Lyssa just could not fathom why Julius felt the need to tell her anything. He had not shared a single detail about Hunter before this moment. Julius had always been so careful not to speak too much of his mission. Why in the world would he feel the need to mention it now?

"I just thought you'd want to know." He looked at her perceptively. He was right. A part of her wanted to know that Hunter cared, even though she knew she should not want to.

"Okay. Now I know."

"He'll be home soon, Lyssa."

"Uh huh." She answered him without really hearing what he was saying. "Are we done here? I have some portals to find." Lyssa picked at her fingernails and examined the spaces between where her fingers met her hands. Since Julius did not respond, she knew that she was reprieved.

When she went back home, she saw that the locket now lay on her pillow. Was this Hunter's way of telling her that he still wanted her? She picked up the locket and turned it over. There was something different about it. On the other side there were words now engraved.

I love you forever and always.

When she opened the locket, she almost dropped it. Instead of Hunter's smiling face, the picture of the boy in her vision was smiling back at her. On the other side was a small picture of a wedding that had not taken place yet. Lyssa saw his face smiling next to hers. She closed it quickly and sat down on the bed, still fingering the locket. Lyssa took a deep breath, then opened it again. This time there were no pictures inside.

Lyssa. She heard his voice drift across the breeze blowing through the window behind her. It was a desperate plea meant for her ears alone. Biting her bottom lip, she tried to keep herself from replying, but somehow even that could not hold her back. She placed the necklace around her neck and felt the protective glow of energy swarm around her. His energy. The part of him that made her feel close to him, the beat of his heart, the smile of his mouth near hers. He was still there in the darkness.

Hunter. It was a simple reply, because she didn't know what else she could possibly have to say. Lyssa was still drawn to him, even though she had tried desperately to push his memory aside. She would probably always be drawn to him, whether it made sense or not. Now was not the time to stand around waiting to hear more. It was time to get moving, time to forget the voice that tried to pull her closer to it. She needed to do something else to distract her from the sadness that was fighting its way back into her heart. Lyssa pulled out her black clothing and got ready for her journey through the next portal, ignoring the warning chills that permeated the air. There was a job to do, and nothing else mattered.

Chapter 23

At this point in time, there were several choices of portals to explore. Imagining one spot on the map, she teleported there easily. When she looked up, she sucked in her breath. Grand Boulevard. It had been a lifetime since she had been there. The last time was when she had seen *Phantom of the Opera* at the Fox Theatre. Walking down the sidewalk, the marquee to the theatre lit up every inch of the night around her.

The vortex of the portal could be felt from where she stood, and she was immediately drawn to the alley behind the theatre. Lyssa tried not to stand out from the crowd of people gathering for the next show as she cut into the alley quickly, turned to make sure she was not being followed, and then continued down the alley. A strong energy threatened the stillness around her when she reached a dumpster past the theatre doors that exited into the alley.

Moving behind the dumpster, she put a hand out to feel for the portal. When a blast of cold air hit her, Lyssa knew it was right in front of her. She closed her eyes, took a deep breath, and walked into it. At once, her body was sucked through a long wind tunnel as she crossed through to the other side, but moving through it had taken much longer than the first portal. When she reached the other side, she was standing in an alley much like the one she had just left, with only one exit. Yanking her hood down lower, she walked slowly down the alley to the exit in front of her. When Lyssa turned the corner, she saw that this was definitely a different area of the Land of the Shadows. Before Lyssa advanced any further, she brought out her wand to create the energy cloak that blocked her trail from the shadows.

No roads presented in front of her, only blackened waterways that were covered in boats shaped much like gondolas. Some were moving on their own accord, others were being steered by shadows gripping oars that moved eerily in the water. There were buildings on either side of the waterways and bridges joining one area to the next. This was very reminiscent of Venice, but the buildings were much more modern with their sharp edges and glass that jutted out almost threateningly to the air around it. Here, there were no black ashes falling around her, just black clouds that circulated like mini tornadoes around the tops of the buildings. Every once in a while, flashes of light slammed through one cloud to another, making her think that some of the shadows were fighting within the menacing masses of air, as if they were trapped within while clawing their way out with every bit of force they had. Had those clouds carried up shadows through the eye of a tornado? How many were trapped within the masses? Lyssa had to keep moving, for she feared that those tornadoes would move at any moment and catch more prey within the eye of their storms. Perhaps that was why the shadows were moving farther away from this area.

These shadows were certainly more corporeal than the last, as she could see the muscles moving through the blackness as they maneuvered their boats through the gentle current of the river. Their shapes were defined all the way from their heads down to their toes in a seamless fashion. Yes, these shadows were more advanced than any of the ones they had ever encountered.

All the boats seemed to be navigating in the same direction. If she wanted to find more information, she would have to follow them, and since she did not think swimming was an option, she would have to find a boat that was unoccupied. She waited as boat after boat passed, keeping her head down and fading into the background of the building behind her.

When she finally saw a boat drifting down the river with no occupant, she moved closer to the water. It was a few inches away from the edge of the dock when she leaned over the edge and reached for it. The current was strong, pulling the boat so forcefully that she had to pull hard to get it to line up with the dock. She climbed inside of it and grabbed onto both sides until the bobbing waves settled beneath her. Lyssa really did not want to fall into the water, for there was no telling what lay in its depths.

Reaching for the oars attached to the sides of the boat, she began to steer through the murky waters, following the boats in front of her as she continued to look back up at the clouds circling over her. Lyssa felt the air moving behind her and saw the tail of a smaller tornado moving closer to the water. She sliced the oars through the water as fast as she could to get away from the cloud, but as she looked back, she realized that it had touched down and was moving back up into the sky. Her first thoughts had been correct, for the tornado had sucked up a handful of shadows from the boats behind her. Lyssa heard screams that she imagined were much like the shrieks of a haunting banshee as the tornado-like clouds continued to transport the black essences upward.

The aftermath of the wind made the waves of the river shake her boat so hard, she thought it would capsize. Lyssa threw the oars inside the boat and clung to the sides so hard she could see the whites of her knuckles. She was lucky that the tornadoes left as quickly as they came. Looking up to the sky, she took a deep calming breath, for the waters had stilled. She pulled out the oars once more and paddled faster than before, attempting to put distance between her and those clouds.

The boat moved faster, and when she made it to the end of the stream, it branched off into another. The current in this stream was highly accelerated, so less rowing was required. She used the oars to steer her way down the new stream. When she saw shadows docking their boats up ahead, she knew there had to be some kind of meeting place near here.

When she neared the dock, the boat seemed to know to stop. Lyssa couldn't help thinking how bizarre this was, but had to remind herself that this world was powered with a magic that was completely different than her own. The rules of her world probably did not apply to this one.

Climbing onto the dock, she quickly dodged to the side of the closest building. The shadows were moving down the path between two buildings farther down. It was imperative that she be careful not to get too close to them, so while her instincts wanted to race after them, logic replaced them. She walked slowly with her head turned to the ground and as quietly as her feet would move her. Lyssa remembered to turn around ever so slowly to see if any other shadows followed behind her, but since the tornadoes had eaten a few of the ones behind her earlier, there were no shadows there. It would be safe to continue.

When she made it down the walkway in front of her, she saw an area that looked much like a garden with many different sculptures. She walked closer and saw that the shadows were gathered around a black orb in the middle of the courtyard below her. The garden surrounded the courtyard like an old amphitheater. The grass around her was gray, and some of the flowers around her sprouted black petals, while others were shades of grey. When she bent to pick up a flower, it shriveled under her touch. She moved quickly away from it, hoping that the shadows had not noticed the flower react to her touch. She was sure her energy had pulsed through to the petal itself and caused a reaction that she had not expected.

Continuing down the path, she did her best to mimic their floating movement. Lyssa felt she was failing miserably, but it became clear that they were too absorbed in what they were doing to notice her.

Lyssa moved on to another area of the garden, because something was pulling her closer. When she passed through a wrought iron gate, she almost gasped aloud. This garden was covered in black marble statues that were unlike any that she had seen before. These were statues of people, all in different defensive poses, with a horrific look of terror carved deeply into each face. One could not imitate this emotion; any carving would pale in comparison to the reality of an actual human form. That was when she realized that these statues were souls lost to the shadow world.

When the first echoing thoughts were floating on the wind, she was the only one who seemed to notice. *Please help, let us go, get us out of here.* The messages played a bittersweet symphony in her head, but since she knew the shadows would feel her if she acted, Lyssa held herself back. There was no way she could defend herself against all of the shadows gathered in the courtyard behind her. She vowed to come back to free them when she had figured out how to combat the evil magic created from the obsidian orbs below. Not one of them was Lana, and Lyssa had started to feel like she would never find her soul to set her free.

Lyssa looked down at her feet when she felt the rocks moving underneath them. Mixed among the white rocks below were tiny obsidian fragments that were apparently picking up her living energy. She reached down, picked up a few of these black stones, and quickly pocketed them. They started to bounce around inside her pockets, so she put a hand inside and held them still. If she could find something to destroy these rocks, perhaps they could destroy the orbs that powered the demon shadows that fed on their world. She quickly teleported out of the world and found herself safely ensconced in her room once more.

After placing the rocks on the dresser, she sat on her bed to reflect on what she had learned tonight. Every portal led to a different place, and not all of these places were friendly to the shadows, as the tornadoes had clearly devoured some of them in front of her. One thing had remained consistent. The shadows were drawn to the mysterious obsidian orbs in their worlds. They gained power from them and used the energy from trapped souls to continuously send power into these orbs. These small rocks seem to be made from the same substance. They still moved every once in a while, making small rocking motions against the grain of the wood. Lyssa would wait until morning to explore the composition of the rocks and find what elements might break them.

Chapter 24

Lyssa had decided not to tell Julius about her journey through the portal the night before. She wanted to learn more about the rocks she had gathered before she handed them over. Her morning had been spent testing different liquid compositions on them, but nothing seemed to work. Water made them bounce higher in the air. She tried rubbing alcohol, peroxide, cough syrup, and anything she could pull out of the medicine cabinet. When those did not work, she pulled chemicals found in cleansers. None of that worked to break down the rocks either; in fact, all it did was shine the rocks so that they gleamed wickedly at her.

It was then that she decided to sneak into the chemistry lab at school. After teleporting there, she ran through so many chemicals, that she lost track of which ones and how many she had used. All she knew was that none of them seemed to work. When she heard footsteps outside the door, she quickly returned to her room.

Lyssa went to the kitchen and pulled down a pan to set them in. Then she turned on the oven to the highest setting and slid the pan inside. She turned on the oven light so that she could keep an eye out for any reaction to the heat. She must have sat by the oven for an hour before she decided to pull them out. When she pulled the pan out, the rocks were unchanged. As she moved her fingers over them, she was surprised to find no heat emanating from them. Lyssa took a chance and touched one of the rocks, only to find that it was freezing cold. *How bizarre.*

Next, Lyssa placed the pan in the freezer to see what kind of effect the cold would have on them. She carefully piled other frozen foods around them to hide them from Jackson. Part of her wanted to tell him everything she had learned, but she did not want to add to his stress right now. He was in the middle of designing costumes for his first show and under a lot of stress. Throw in his duties with the Watch Tower, and he was stretched way beyond most people's limits.

After leaving the rocks in the freezer, she went to the library to do some more work for the Watch Tower. The hours spent trying to find these portals and shadows were becoming monotonous. She was thankful that Julius had sent her through the portals. It gave her something else to focus on.

Lyssa ran her finger over the locket around her neck and let it fall back into place. Things always had to be complicated, didn't they? Nothing in life had ever been easy. From the moment she was born into this world, she'd had to learn to fight for her life. Sometimes she just got tired of the battle. Sometimes she wanted the simplest answer to make life smooth like a glass pond…no ripples, no waves, just peace. Lyssa had thought she was achieving it several months before, but pebbles interrupted the stillness, and there was no calming the movement of the rings across the surface.

She pushed her thoughts away. They did not belong there. There was probably a better time and place for them. Much like Hunter, she had a job to do, and nothing and no one else should interrupt that.

Lyssa spent another hour working on cataloging her findings before she headed back home and went to the kitchen to check on the rocks. When she pulled them out of the freezer, they'd had the opposite reaction in the freezer. There were puddles pooling around the bottom of the freezer, because the rocks had started to heat up the air around them. She removed them carefully from the freezer and set them on the counter to her right. Within moments the oozing rocks hardened into flat stones.

Lyssa pulled out a kitchen mallet from the drawer and started to smash at them. When she looked to see if they were damaged, she could see that they were unaffected. "Seriously?"

Lyssa picked them up and put them in her pocket, then headed back to her room. What else could she try? She pulled out her backpack of magical items and placed them one at a time on the dresser in front of her. She put each object near the rocks to see if there were any reactions. Amethyst? No reaction. Quartz crystal. Nothing. When she put the rose quartz near them, the rocks hummed disturbingly. Lyssa pulled the rock away and looked at it, puzzled. What was it about this rose quartz that made these rocks respond in such a way? Rose quartz wasn't particularly powerful. She used it when she wanted to feel peace and love surround her. They brought her happiness. "Wait a minute...that's it!"

Lyssa put the rose quartz in her hand in front of her and imagined the calmest, warmest, fuzziest thoughts possible. She was having trouble bringing those close to the surface, possibly due to the melancholy that she was feeling. She had to do something if she wanted to prove her theory. Lyssa opened her thoughts and put her hand on her locket. *Hunter?*

Lyssa? Are you all right? It had taken a moment for him to answer, but clearly he did not want to push her further away.

I'm fine. It's just...well, I love you. It was hard to say at first, but she felt that she needed to say it, needed to believe that the feelings they had for each other could still be there, even after all this time.

I love you, always and forever. She felt the peace and love flow through her from his locket. It made her smile, and she sent the warm tingly feelings into the rose quartz. When she felt it vibrating loudly in her hand, she channeled it into a pink orb of light in front of her. She sent the orb crashing into the rock and watched as it shattered into dust around her.

"Really? That's it? Love? Peace, happy thoughts? That would annihilate the power that feeds these monsters?" Lyssa put the rose quartz back into her bag, then picked up the other rock and made her way back down to the library. When she saw that the room was empty, she went in search of Julius to share her findings with him.

He was in the atrium at the back of the house. Lyssa nodded at him to get his attention, and he quickly finished the task he was working on so that he could meet her in the library.

He came into the room moments after she had entered it. "We'll need some privacy."

Julius made the same precautions that he had before. "What did you find?"

"I went into a different portal last night, the one in St. Louis. I found the shadows pulling energy from another orb just like the last portal. There were souls trapped there too, but they were frozen in statue-like forms. Near those souls, I found smaller bits of the rock that the orbs are made of. It looks very much like obsidian to me." She pulled the rock out of her pocket and pushed it to him.

"Interesting."

"It gets better. I tried to use everything I could find against these rocks. It does not respond to chemicals, to heat, or to cold."

"Did you find anything that it did respond to?"

Lyssa pulled out the rose quartz from her bag and placed it near the rock. Julius almost jumped out of his seat as the black stone shot as fast as it could in the opposite direction of the quartz. "What in the world?"

"It hates rose quartz, and do you know why?"

He blew air out of his mouth as he tried to contemplate what made rose quartz such an adversary to the obsidian. "Not off the top of my head."

"These rocks deal very much in energy. They siphon energy, store energy, give off energy. The energy that feeds them is the despair, negativity, depression, and darkest thoughts of others. When you think about it, rose quartz stores the polar opposite. These stones are storing peace, tranquility, and the most powerful feeling of all. Love." Lyssa had learned about these rocks from Lana's coven. While completely unobtrusive to most people, the peaceful nature of the rocks was actually quite powerful. Lyssa wondered if Lana had figured out the connection of these rocks to the shadows. Was that why the Craven had killed her?

"So to fight the energy feeding those shadows, we need to channel a different energy into their world."

"In a matter of speaking. We could use this energy to destroy the orbs and perhaps shut down the portals. This may only be a temporary fix to the situation, for I have not begun any tests on the orbs within the Land of the Shadows. I have only tested it on these rocks."

"We'll need much more evidence in order to get more of the Watch Tower to assist us."

"I realize that. I'm going back in tonight." Part of her knew that she should not attempt this alone, but the pigheaded part of her decided she could do this. She would take down this orb and prove that these shadows could be stopped once and for all.

"Be careful, Lyssa. Don't take any unnecessary actions."

"Of course." He did not need to know that she would take any action necessary to bring down these shadows. Too many people had suffered. Too much damage had already been done.

Chapter 25

Tonight, Lyssa was going back to the last portal that she had visited. She had spent some time drawing a map of the world, so that once she entered the portal, she could teleport directly to the orb without attracting the tornado clouds from the sky. If she waited until the witching hour, then most of the shadows would be vacant from their world.

When she entered the portal, she pulled out the map and ran her fingers over it. Lyssa had only been able to create the areas that she had explored. There was a chance that orbs were in other places as well, but she was going with what she already knew from her first exploration. While she was going to try to take down the orb, she was also testing a theory out to free the souls trapped within the rock garden.

Lyssa ran her fingers over the map and waited to see if she could feel the energy trail that the shadows left. She could not sense any activity in the garden areas. There was activity in areas of the map that had not been drawn yet, but not nearly close enough for her to worry about. Taking a deep breath, she gathered as much courage as she could and teleported to the where the obsidian orb was located.

It was even darker in the garden tonight. She was now standing in the middle of the courtyard, and when she looked up, she could see where she had stood the other day. Moving closer to the orb, she reached her hand out to touch it. One woman's screams of agony roared through her head, and she moved her hand away.

Lyssa placed both hands to her temple to help sway the painful flashes she saw in her mind. Lana. She had been too late to save her soul. Lyssa curled her fingers into tight balls and squeezed her eyes shut when other screams started to filter through the silence. Apparently, this orb held all the pain and memories of each and every one of its victims and had taken so many souls, it was hard to separate one from another. Soon she was overwhelmed with the emotions that swarmed around her. It became clear to her that it would be better not to touch another orb in the future if she could avoid it. She could not afford to be distracted by the feelings stored within them.

Pulling out the large rose quartz, she put every inch of her hopes and dreams into it. Lyssa imagined the face of the child in her future and grabbed onto her locket, but it was not enough. She took a deep breath and let every sad, angry, and belligerent thought leave her body. Lyssa imagined Jackson's smiling face and felt his warmth run through her, for he had always been the best part of her life. Then she imagined Lana's sarcastic voice teasing her as she often did. When she held enough courage within her, she tried to see Hunter's face without remembering the pain of their separation. She had to lock up those emotions, for right now she needed to simply exist within the happiness of the memory of his embrace.

The rose quartz hummed loudly in her hand, and she knew she had charged it as much as she possibly could. Lyssa created a large white light that she suspended in the air before her. When it had grown to the size of the orb, her mind forced it toward its black counterpart. The light merged and melted into the darkness before her.

The energy she sent into the orb started to create cracks within its design, almost as if the light were seeping through the darkness. She heard a hiss as the light splintered, and the black orb looked much like a parched riverbank in the middle of a hot drought, its cracks trembling loudly. She watched it glow like an ember in a flame before it cracked one last time. For an instant, she thought that energy she had filtered into it had done all that it would, and she was disappointed that she had not been able to affect it more. Then suddenly she was ducking her head, trying to avoid the exploding orb as it sent shards into the air upon ignition.

Lyssa was not fast enough, and she felt something hot rip across her head. She ducked to the ground, gripping her head as the rest of the orb detonated around her. When she pulled her hand away from the back of her head, it was covered in blood. Lyssa attempted to apply more pressure to still the bleeding, but the world was fading around her as she murmured the only thing she could. *Hunter!*

Her head was pounding like a jackhammer when she woke up just moments later. The incessant throbbing made it hard to focus her eyes. When she was finally able to, she looked through squinting eyes at the world around her. The shadows swarmed around her, and she knew they would have her in moments if she didn't do something quickly. She grabbed her wand out of her bag and aimed at the growing darkness surrounding her.

They were so close together, it was hard to tell where one shadow started and the other began. Their icy black fingertips pulled at every inch of her, and she felt herself being pulled deeper into their blackness. Pulling the locket off her neck, she gripped it within her fingers. The shadows tried to pull her apart piece by piece, but she would not break. Lyssa used all the energy she had left inside her and made a shield full of light to surround her. They raised their crystals and started blasting at her until she flew through the air and crashed onto the ground a few feet away. She felt them breaking through the shield and cried out one last time. "Hunter!" Her scream pierced the air around her as the shadows floated closer towards her. One last blast, and they had annihilated her shield. She curled up in a ball and prepared herself for an attack. It never came.

Suddenly, there were three other guardians surrounding her, their wands raised and ready for the approaching shadows. She tried to keep her eyes open, but the pain in the back of her head finally took the little energy that she had left. Lyssa let her head fall back to the ground, and the last sight she saw before darkness hit was Hunter's angry face.

Chapter 26

When she came to, her head was swimming, and dots were clouding her vision. Lyssa tried to speak, but no words would come out. She brought her hand to her forehead and felt bandages wrapped tightly around it.

Jackson rushed to her side. "Careful, Lyssa. We don't want to damage Sarah's fine work." He nodded to the blonde in the corner.

Sarah rose and came to the other side of her bed. She lifted a light scope to look in Lyssa's eyes. "Do you see the light?"

Before the light had flashed in her pupils, Lyssa saw the number 12 tattooed on her left forearm. Lyssa tried to move her mouth and form the words, but her mouth was parched. When she attempted a nod, a blinding pain bit into the back of her head. She must have gotten hit harder than she thought. Lyssa moved her eyes around the room, searching for Hunter.

"He's okay, Lyssa. He had to go back. We're all fine. It's you we're worried about, going off all half-assed like that without taking any of us with you." He was clearly upset at her.

Lyssa smirked at him and pursed her lips. Attitude must have shown quickly on her face, because Sarah started to chuckle. "Cool it there, buddy. Yelling at my patient is not going to help the situation. Listen to me, Lyssa. You've been asleep for three days, and we're not quite done with our healing rituals. I'm going to have to put you in a longer sleep, more like a meditation than a coma. It might take a couple of days, maybe a week. When you wake up, you'll be as good as new. Do you understand? No, don't try to nod again please. Just raise one finger for yes, two for no."

Lyssa made a fist in her right hand and opened just one finger. She understood what Sarah was saying. The healers would be patching her up while she slept, and although she had just woken up, she was still exhausted. If she could wake up without such a pounding headache, that would be so much better. Lyssa smiled at them and winked at Serena, who was looking at her with tears in her eyes. When Sarah moved her hands over her head, she felt her eyelids get heavy. Sarah's healing energy was all she felt before she nodded off once again.

The next time she woke, Hunter was by her bedside, crouched over the hand that he held. She squeezed his hand lightly, and he raised his head. He looked like every ounce of his being was in mourning, but for what, she had no idea. "Lyssa."

"Hunter," she whispered back. It was all she could manage, considering she had not used her vocal chords for an extended period of time. "What day is it?"

"October 25."

What? That much time had passed? That meant she had been in bed for almost two months. She saw gemstones surrounding her bed and could tell they had been working overtime to help bring her back to the land of the living.

"I'll be right back, Lyssa." Hunter left the room and returned quickly with Sarah.

"Ah, there's my patient. It seems you needed longer than we first thought to recover from that head wound. Let's get some food and water in you. Hunter, you can come back later when we have sorted her out here." He did not want to leave. It was clear that he wanted to argue with Sarah, but she was having none of it. She pointed to the door and commanded him to get out once again.

"Okay, dear Lyssa. Let's get your voice together for you. I know you'll have questions to ask, so first, let's get those vocal chords hydrated."

Lyssa spent the next two hours getting checked over for residual damage. Her vocal chords were in working order before long. It was hard to move her legs at first, but when Sarah applied a warming poultice of some concoction she had put together in the mixing bowl in front of her, the life seemed to seep right back into her limbs. Lyssa sat up and tried to push herself out of the bed.

"Whoa there. None of that yet. Just focus on keeping the energy flowing through those legs right now, if you please."

Jackson had come in to fill her in on what had been happening around them while she was asleep. The Watch Tower was putting her strategies into play; and with the documented portals that she had detailed in her reports, they were destroying more orbs around the world. While this was happening, Hunter and Logan remained within the heart of the Craven, finding new leads and information for taking down the organization once and for all. Hunter was coming to see her during times that did not coincide with his movements within the Craven. For all intents and purposes, everything was going as planned, even in her absence. The summer session had just ended at school when she was injured, and Lyssa had not yet signed up for any fall classes. So for now, she did not have to worry about that stress.

When Sarah finally left the room, Hunter entered quietly. He looked at her face, and she could tell that these two months had been difficult on him. "Why are you here?" she couldn't help asking. Lyssa knew he was supposed to be deep undercover.

"Why?" Hunter shook his head in disbelief. "Why do you think I am here, Lyssa? I have to be here. I need to see for myself that you are okay."

"I'm on the mend, Hunter. We both still have jobs to do. I've already put yours in jeopardy. I'm sorry." There was deep remorse in her voice. She just hoped that she had not blown his cover. His work was so important to their cause. Lyssa could never forgive herself if she ruined his identity within the Craven.

"You almost lost your life, and you want to talk about our duties to the Watch Tower? Seriously?"

"Like you have room to talk, Hunter. Your life is in jeopardy every time you leave. It's no different for me. Besides, what else is there to talk about right now? Isn't that all that matters? The work we're doing? It's the most important thing." Lyssa closed her thoughts to him. She did not need him to read the sadness that was tearing her up inside, for she knew she had to send him away. Lyssa could not let him sacrifice his mission for another single day.

Hunter ran his fingers through his hair, and it was clear that he was agitated. "I can't do this anymore." He walked out of the room, and tears ran down her eyes. She had expected this.

By the end of the week, she was itching to get up and moving. Lyssa went into the library and found several guardians around the spinning globe in the middle of the room. They raised their heads and smiled in her direction when she entered.

Julius rose from his chair and walked over to pat her on the back. "Good to have you back."

"What are you working on?" Lyssa walked over to the globe and saw that they were looking over different cities in the country.

"We're going to work on the West Coast right now. There are a few portals in Washington that they wanted to start with."

"When do we leave?"

"We leave tomorrow evening. You should get some more rest before we send you out again."

"Unless you can put me on lock down, I'm going with you. As long as I am not alone, I will be fine."

It was agreed that she would be going with them the next evening. Lyssa teleported to her room to gather her thoughts for the journey ahead. She was glad to see that the information she had gleaned from her previous excursions was proving useful to the Watch Tower. The fact that she had been able to help in the fight against the shadows on her world warmed her heart.

Lyssa was going through her closet to make sure she had the right clothing for tomorrow when she heard a whoosh of air in the room.

"Lyssa, you are not going to the Land of the Shadows without me."

"Wow, you're barely in here for a minute, and you want to put your balls to the wall. News flash, Hunter…you do not control what I do. I'm a grown woman. I can take care of myself."

"Like last time?"

"Last time was my fault. I took on too much alone. I'll be fine with the others there."

"You can't do this. Please, you need to regain your strength. You could get yourself injured so badly that you won't make it back."

"You don't get to tell me what to do. You don't get to tell me anything. Who the hell do you think you are? If you haven't noticed, you've been out of my life so long, it was like you were never in it. What right do you think you have to control anything I do? We're not together, are we?"

"Wait here while I go talk to Julius. I know he put you up to this, just like he put you up to your other excursions. I'm done with this. It's over."

"Do your worst, Hunter. You still won't stop me." But he had already disappeared from her room. This was a disaster. Her stupid foolish emotions had gotten the best of her again. She had not meant to fight with him, but he really did not have the right to dictate her actions. Her mind settled on his last words to her. Did he mean that they were over? How would that be any different than their current hiatus?

Lyssa sat on her bed and waited for him to come back, but Hunter did not return as soon as she thought. She lay down on her bed and curled up in a ball, the most comfortable position when the whole world continued to be turned upside down. Lyssa tried to fight the exhaustion that felt like lead pulling down against the gravity of her eyelids. She drifted to sleep trying to hold on to the image of the family that she had seen in the vision, a family that at one point had seemed like a destiny worth fighting for.

Chapter 27

Hunter did not return that night, and for the first time in forever, she slept until dawn's light was just starting to trickle through her window. When she finally left her room, the apartment was empty. Usually Jackson would be sitting in the living room or the kitchen, but no one was anywhere to be found.

After making herself a quick meal, she teleported to the library to do some more searching. Lyssa spent a few hours scanning the globe for more activity and charting her findings, and discovered at least six areas where she could sense active portals. She was so caught up in what she was doing she did not hear anyone enter the room.

"Lyssa?"

She turned to see Hunter standing behind her in clothes that appeared to be wet. "What happened to you?" Lyssa was completely avoiding the questions that she wanted to ask. What happened last night? What did you tell Julius? All of the things she was afraid to know the answer to.

"You should see this." He pushed the button to get the screen from the ceiling and turned it on.

Lyssa was surprised to see that a vehicle had crashed into the railing of a river near her college. The car had been pulled up from the water, but the driver was missing. A photograph came onto the screen, and she gasped aloud. It looked like

Hunter, but it was off just slightly. "It's you. Or it was you? What exactly does this mean?"

"This is how the Craven saw me. I used a glimmer charm to hide my true identity. Anyone who knew me could see me the way that I actually am. This man, Charles Darvinger, was the man that was moving up within their ranks. It means that this Charles Darvinger is no longer with the living, or at least that is what the Craven thinks."

"But how? Does this mean that...?"

"I'm off the case? Yes. Yes it does." A little more life crawled back into his face as a soft smile started to fill it.

A desire to throw her arms around him filled her, but she felt the guilt holding her back. If she was the reason this mission failed and more people died because of it, she would never forgive herself. Lyssa sat at the table and hunched her shoulders over. Hunter could not leave his mission. They needed him and Logan to get as close to the inner workings of the Craven as possible. That factor had never changed.

"Oh, get up and hug him already, you dolt." Serena had been watching from the doorway.

Lyssa looked up at her, and her eyebrows raised unexpectedly. "What in the world is going on?"

"Hunter, you better take her somewhere else and fill her in on what happened last night. She'll definitely want to hear it."

Hunter walked over to her and reached for her hand. Lyssa took it cautiously and looked up into his face just before he started to lower his mouth to hers. When his lips reached hers, they were soaring through the air, to where, she had no idea. When they finally stopped, she pulled away from him and looked around. It was the house in the vision that she'd had before. "Hunter? Where are we?"

"Home. Or the one that my parents used to own. It's been mine since they passed three years ago." He answered her so calmly that she had to look at him again. "Come inside, Lyssa. We need to talk."

Lyssa followed him inside and winced as the screen door hit the frame, slamming shut in the silence around them. Avoiding eye contact, she stared at each wall in turn. It was easier than looking at Hunter right now. They were standing in the family room, where two chairs sat near the big window at the front of the room, separated by a table and a few floor lamps. On the other side of the room was a long sectional couch in a shade of butter cream suede. The walls were a peaceful blue, and its calming hue made her feel almost comforted. Hunter sat down on the couch and gestured for her to sit down. She debated sitting in one of the armchairs across from it, but decided now was not a good time to start acting like a chicken. Lyssa did sit, but at the furthest end away from him.

"Stop acting like you're in trouble, Lyssa."

"Hunter, you can't tell me that this is the way that the mission was supposed to go. How are we going to find the information that we needed? All those people were depending on us, and all for naught. It's so selfish."

Hunter smiled at her. "There are two people in that equation, Lyssa. I chose to leave the mission. You never asked me to. I'd do it again."

"Sure, you say that now. Wait until it all hits the fan. Then you'll regret it."

"No, you don't get to decide how I'll feel. Only I do. And I won't. Logan is quite capable of getting the information that we need, and having one new person at a time is less conspicuous. It's actually better. Better for the mission, better for you, and definitely better for me." He moved closer to her, and she was suddenly aware they were alone.

Lyssa still tried to shake off what he was telling her. "You can't just make the decisions for me. I should have had a say in this."

"Very well. What would you have said?"

"I would have told you that there were others who counted on us to do our jobs, even if I didn't want you to go. Why did you come back for me?"

"Because you called." His eyes met hers, and the distance seemed minimal. He put his hand on her neck and stroked her hair softly. This time when he moved closer, she was prepared for Hunter's lips on hers. Hunter responded faster than she anticipated, and a sweet tender kiss turned into something entirely more intimate. She felt the racing heart under her fingers as she laced her hands in his shirt.

Before she knew it, they were moving through the air once again. "Where are we now?"

"Upstairs."

"We could have walked, you know." When she dared to open her eyes, she found that they were inside their room, the one place where passion was unencumbered, and they were not at odds with the world. "Hunter?"

"Yes?"

"We've been coming to your house all this time?" He was starting a trail of kisses down her neck, and she was finding it very hard to focus on all the questions that she had for him. When he picked her up and carried her to the bed, she gave up.

"Hunter?"

"Hmm?" He still did not look up at her as his finger played around with a button on her shirt.

"What are you doing?"

"Well if you have to ask, I must be out of practice." He now had all the buttons free and was running a finger lightly down her stomach. She sucked in her gut when his hand reached below her navel. While she had been sitting there as if she was a spectator, she suddenly felt it would be in her best interest to pay attention to what Hunter was doing. Before she knew it, she lay completely naked before him, and in the light of the day, she felt insecure. Lyssa tried to look away from his inquiring gaze, but he stopped her.

"Don't look away, Lyssa. Look here." He pointed to his eyes. Lyssa sucked in a brave breath and looked in his eyes. "I see you better than you see yourself." His eyes were alight with something much deeper than desire. She kept her eyes on him as he ran his hands down her body, every single inch he traveled sending delicious chills up and down her skin. His touch was so gentle, and desire fluttered inside her like a slow wind that threatened to turn into a delicious storm of energy. She tried to reach up to assist him with his own clothing, but he pushed her hands away.

"Not yet. There's plenty of time."

His answer echoed the sentiments of moments before. He would take his time because he was not going anywhere. He was choosing to be by her side. Hunter was choosing her, and when this thought finally hit home, it was liberating.

Lyssa left her reservations at the foot of the bed as he made love to her body with his hands and mouth, each delicious wave of desire running through her in slow motion until she started to crave the feel of his flesh on hers. She dug her way out of the passion filled cloud that was storming around her. Grabbing his shirt, she pulled him closer to her, and when he refused to budge, she heard the rip of fabric under her fingertips.

Hunter caught her hands in his and chuckled. "Yes, ma'am." He quickly removed his shirt, and she felt his intake of breath as his chest moved under her fingertips. When she ran one of her nails over his nipple, he tried to push her hand away and moved ever so slowly away from her body.

"Turn around." His voice cut through the haze. She sat up and turned around slowly, eyeing him with curiosity as she turned. He gently touched the scar on the back of her head, and she could feel a brief bout of sadness fall between them. When the first kiss fell on her neck and started to run down her shoulders, she arched her back into him, forgetting any sadness in the world. His hands reached around to caress her breasts as his hot skin melted into her back. She tilted her head back for a kiss that made her feverish. There they sat when the gentle tide took her away and melted her in his hands and his lips. Lyssa could not fight the desire that ran through her. To deny it would be to deny herself the air she breathed.

Hunter lowered her back onto the bed, and the heat in his eyes told her that he would not be able to hold back his own needs for much longer. She reached down to the bulge showing through his pants and licked her lips when he bucked against her hand. He removed the rest of his clothing quickly and lowered himself onto her. Lyssa wrapped her arms around him and breathed in the scent of him. She could tell he was holding himself back as he continued to stoke her fires with a skill that simply amazed her.

His erection was pulsing close to her legs, and she ached for it. It rocked back and forth, touching her nether lips so achingly, yet not getting close enough to the entrance to fulfill the deepest part of her. Lyssa knew he would stop soon, but she ached to feel him inside her. She wrapped her legs around him and enticed him to enter her, then distracted his conscience with a kiss that made them both senseless as she pulled him into her.

Hunter pulled his mouth away, and his breath caught in his throat. She knew he was trying to reason through the madness, but she wouldn't let him. While she had enjoyed their lovemaking before, this was so much more intense, for she had not felt the full heat of him inside her the other times. When he trusted himself to move within her, she felt wave after wave of delicious release that had been trapped beneath the surface. The beat of their hearts kept time with the rhythm of their bodies falling into each other over and over again. There was nothing keeping them from feeling, no distracting the finish that made the stars explode behind their eyes.

"Lyssa, I didn't—"

"Don't worry so much. I've got it covered." Lyssa felt him still buried deep within her, and she was still pulsing around him. He moved slowly again, and she moaned. Soon they were caught up in each other again, and they finished again as she held him closer to her.

She sat there with her thoughts swirling around. They had just had the most amazing sex, but her thoughts that she had pushed to the farthest reaches of her mind climbed forward. Hunter could still have jeopardized everything they had been working for just to be with her. "Hunter, I—" she started to say. She felt like she needed to apologize for making him feel like he had no other choice.

"Don't say you're sorry. I'm not. I'm right where I want to be."

Tears started to crowd the corners of her eyes. If things weren't so messed up with the world, she would feel so carefree at the moment. She snuggled against him and nuzzled his neck with her nose. "Me too."

Elissa Daye

Chapter 28

Lyssa woke up to the smell of something tasty being cooked below. Pulling on her clothes, she went to the mirror to inspect the chaos that used to be her hair. She did the best she could to straighten it with her fingers, but it was a painful process. Finally giving up, she decided to leave it the way it was.

Before climbing down the stairs, she decided to look around the house. Down the hallway, she found three other bedrooms, one of which was actually the master bedroom. Lyssa wondered why Hunter did not use this room, since it had a large adjoining bathroom, but then she realized this had to be his parents' room. It was still decorated with their things, small odds and ends collected on vacations, picture frames that lay untouched on the shelves and walls. She could understand how hard it must be to let go of the happiness he must have had with his family, but part of her wished that she could relate.

Placing one hand on the railing, she climbed down the stairs. She let her nose find its way to the kitchen and found it to be at the back of the house on the first floor. Hunter was busy stirring something on the stove when she reached her arms around him. He stopped what he was doing and turned around for her embrace. "Good afternoon."

"Is it really late? Are we in trouble?" She kissed his nose and snuck around him to see what he was cooking.

"Hey, no peeking. And no. We are not in trouble. I informed Julius that we would be taking the next two days off. I need to lie low, just in case they didn't buy my death."

"Then I'm staying here with you, so I can keep an eye on you." After all these months, Lyssa did not want to lose Hunter again. She had almost given up on the idea of him, but she had not been able to let him go. Lyssa pursed her lips thoughtfully as she considered the image of Hunter and the little boy. Was that a life he would consider sharing with her? Would they always want to be with the Watch Tower? Were they always guardians once they started to align with them? Lyssa realized that life was too complicated currently to contemplate these ideas, and she was about to ask, but Hunter beat her to the chase.

"Yes, that life appeals to me very much so, and only with you in it, but right now it's complicated, Lyssa. Please don't misunderstand me. If we're going to make the world a better place for us, make it safer for our own children someday, then we have to find a way to vanquish these shadows from the Earth."

"But if there aren't shadows to fight, there will be something else, like the other things I've sensed on the globe. Surely you know that, Hunter."

"Lyssa, this is the 21st century. Honey, we can have it all if we want. But for now, this will have to be enough. We'll take steps toward a different life when we're ready."

Lyssa left the discussion where it stood. She didn't know why she felt the need to push the issue anyway. It was hard to remind herself to live in the moment and let the future unravel at its own pace, that she did not need to control the outcome every time. Hunter was right. For now there was Hunter and her. The importance of what they were doing was immeasurable, and the journey they took together as they faced it would be well worth it.

While they ate lunch, she noticed that the darkness that had been growing in his face had relaxed, and the old Hunter that she had come to know and love was quickly returning. She offered to help him with the dishes, and they fell in together in an easy silence that felt familiar. As soon as they were finished, they went to sit out on the porch.

"This is a beautiful view." The house was set further away from the city, and they were facing a small lake that was surrounded by tall trees. It was so quiet and peaceful there that she could feel her soul relaxing for a change. It was good to get away from the Watch Tower, even if just for a few days.

Lyssa laid her head on his shoulder and simply took in the moment. This was what life could be like, if they were dealt the right cards. She could sit there forever in the comfort of his arms. Life was getting better every day.

Elissa Daye

Chapter 29

When they returned to the Watch Tower two days later, she felt extremely rested and peaceful. The time with Hunter had been amazing, and while she loved the break, she was anxious to get back to work. Lyssa would not be able to have the life she dreamt of until the guardians had finished their mission to rid their world of the threat Craven and the shadows posed. When she faced the others, she realized that Jackson wasn't there.

"Where's Jackson?"

"About that...well, he wanted to stay to tell you, but when the Elders send you packing, you have to move quickly." Julius looked away uncomfortably. "Don't look so worried, Lyssa. He got a promotion. Jackson really wanted to wait around to tell you and tried to send a magical message, but it seems wherever you were staying was impenetrable to outside magic. Due to his immeasurable ability to take in information, the Elders have made him an archivist. He will be responsible for research that impacts every sector of the Watch Tower."

Lyssa tried to hide her disappointment in his disappearance. It was an amazing opportunity for him, and she had always known the road would fork eventually, leaving them to travel on their separate paths. "So that's that?"

"Don't worry, he's just in training right now. You'll see him soon," offered Serena.

"Okay then." Lyssa shook the cloud of sadness from her mind. "So where to?" She looked over at Julius and the others.

"We have been working on portals on the West Coast in Washington. We were looking at your notes about the Seattle area."

"This area appears to be the worst vortex of negative energy," she told them. "It's one of the top ten cities with the highest suicidal tendencies. I know it's true that the rainy atmosphere there has caused a higher trend in Seasonal Affective Disorder, considering it rains almost all the time, but the shadows have quite a hand in those numbers."

"Agreed." Julius touched the globe and was searching for the portals she had marked on it.

Lyssa leaned over and touched an area in Seattle, but moved her fingers higher up on the map near Puget Sound. The portal she was feeling was close to the water, so she assumed it must have been on the docks near Puget Sound. "Here. This is our best bet."

They gathered their supplies for the trip, taking their biggest rose quartz crystals with them, and teleported to the spot she had indicated on the map. When Lyssa opened her eyes, she was met with a mysterious fog that filled the air with choking sadness. "It's here all right," she said quietly. The ground underneath was a little wobbly as she started walking closer to where she felt the portal nearby. Lyssa looked down to see that she was definitely standing on some makeshift dock that was swaying slightly with the lap of waves against the wood under her feet. She stopped for a moment and let her body adjust to the rocking motion, then moved once she felt her balance returning. The portal was at the end of the dock, and when she put her hand out to feel it, she almost jumped back.

"This is going to be one hell of a fight." Lyssa could tell right away that this particular portal was being held up with more energy than the last few she had gone through. She looked behind her and saw that the guardians were a few paces back. Hunter was nearest to her side. She smiled over at him and stepped into the portal. Even after her last adventures within the portal, she was not afraid to go back in. This time, Lyssa had back up, and she would not be the only force in there against the shadows.

Lyssa pulled out a piece of paper as soon as she entered to start mapping everything she could see. The world around them was actually the calmest she had seen in the Land of the Shadows. It was a small town that appeared as deserted as a ghost town. There were older buildings with wooden sidings, and the sidewalks were more dirt paths than anything else. The world was still cast in hues of black, grey, and white. If she had to compare this part of their world with any of hers, it was reminiscent of the towns she had seen in every old western movie on television as a child. Lyssa half expected to see ghostly cowboys ambling down the streets, holsters hanging from their hips, and the gentle clank of the spurs spinning at their heels. But there was nothing there but a gentle breeze stirring up the dust around them.

"This is certainly unusual." Julius peered around them perplexed.

"No kidding," Serena chimed in.

"Let's mosey along now," chuckled Hunter.

"For such a strong portal, I'd expect more activity inside it. Should we search the buildings?" Lyssa wasn't sure what made her suggest it, for she certainly did not want to start searching them, but part of her felt like she had to offer it up.

She felt more protected out here in the open than she would crowded in the walls of these smaller buildings.

"Do you sense any shadow movement inside?"

Lyssa closed her eyes and let herself read the energy around her. "No. None." Everything seemed eerily quiet to her. "I think we'd be closer to some activity up there near those mountains ahead."

The group agreed with her assessment, and since they were able to see the mountain top destination in front of them, they teleported there instead of spending the hours walking. Once at the top, there was quite a larger clearing than she expected, as this mountain did not appear to have the steep peaks that other mountains seemed to have.

Lyssa walked to the side facing away from the town and peered over the edge. There was a small valley below swarming with shadows, and it looked as if they were having some kind of meet up around a large black orb. That had to be this portal's power source. But how could they get to it with all those shadows guarding it?

"Here." Lyssa pointed over the edge of the mountain. The others came over to view the scene below. "We can't just go in and attack these shadows. They'll be sure to summon more in their wake."

By the frown piercing Julius's face, she could tell he was thinking about the situation at hand. "We can wait a little while. They might be expecting us to attack right now. They may be altering their movement patterns to counter our forces."

"Yeah, but if they keep shadows there at all times, we'll have no choice but to attack them," added Hunter logically.

"I say we wait to see if any of them move away," Serena added.

The Land of the Shadows

The four of them waited for a few hours, just sitting there on the ridge. When Lyssa thought she was going to die from boredom, she saw several of the shadows take off. It looked like it was going to be their hunting time. "Looks like Julius was right. They appear to be moving out now. We'll have to keep changing up our times of attack."

"That, or we'll need to start bringing more guardians with us," Serena suggested. "Let's move. We'll take out the orb first, then attack the shadows."

They all teleported in near the orb, but not close enough to gain the attention of the shadows. Being cloaked certainly had its benefits. After creating shields to protect themselves, each of them pulled out their crystals and started to create orbs of light to send towards the obsidian counterpart in the middle. When their lights had grown large enough to dissolve the orb, they sent them floating at it.

The shadows turned as the light passed them and started to lunge at them. The guardians pulled out their wands, ready for anything they threw at them. Blast after blast of yellow light flew toward the darkness as more shadows came forward. They were almost overwhelmed by the swarming shadows, but they could not move until the orb was destroyed. Wave after wave of blackness pitched around them, but they held their own as the orb shattered before them.

When only a handful of shadows remained, they thought they were ready to teleport out, but suddenly they were surrounded by more than just shadows. Dark figures approached them from all sides. These figures were all dressed in black and carried black obsidian wands in their hands.

"Looks like the Craven are in closer league with these shadows now. We can't handle all this without reinforcements. Another time." Julius nodded at the Craven surrounding them before teleporting out.

The four guardians tried to teleport away as quickly as possible, but as she started to leave, she noticed that Hunter had been trapped between three shadows and four of the Craven. They were holding him down, making it impossible for him to teleport.

"Hunter!" Lyssa sent blast after blast from the fiery tip of her wand. She managed to take down a shadow and one of the Craven standing behind him.

"Lyssa, go!" Hunter's eyes met hers, and his message was clear. "Get out of here now!" The Craven were advancing at her and shadows coming behind her. Lyssa knew he was right, and as the Craven closest to him slammed his fist into Hunter's head, she knew that she could not save him. Lyssa felt her heart rip out of her chest as she teleported away from the clearing.

When she landed in the library behind the others, her knees buckled under her. She fell to the floor, and raised hollow eyes to Julius. "They have him." She felt the world moving around her, but she was stuck in slow motion. She could not hear what they were saying to her, felt only numbness as they tried to get her up into a chair. When she looked around her, her vision was stuck in a narrow tunnel as the world closed in on her. Putting her hand on her locket, she tried to feel Hunter, but his energy was gone. She just sat there, holding her locket in her hand, rubbing it as if she expected a magic genie to come out and take away this horrible nightmare.

Lyssa woke up later to the darkness of her room. She opened her eyes and started to get out of bed as usual. Stretching her arms, Lyssa put one foot in front of the other. She turned around and looked at the empty bed and was instantly reminded of what happened earlier. Hunter. They had him. Was he still alive? As she put her hand around the locket again, tears started to roll down her face, for she could not feel him. *Hunter? Where are you? Hunter*! He never responded. Lyssa could not accept the silence that was slapping her in the face. He was gone, and this time he might not come back.

Elissa Daye

Chapter 30

When the others tried to tell her that Hunter was lost to them, she refused to give up. He could not be. Lyssa would not rest until she found him again. She had spent every moment jumping from one portal to another. When Sector 4 continued their quest to destroy the orbs, Lyssa stayed back, hoping that by focusing on his energy that she would find him. While others had entered a state of mourning, she was in denial. When he was within the Craven's fold before, she had thought she lost him, but the truth was she had never lost him, and she would not lose him now. Lyssa spent hours reliving that moment, wishing that she had stayed to fight against the darkness dragging him down, but she knew that she had a much better chance of finding him if she remained alive. And she would find him. Wouldn't she?

It had been another week before she started to lose hope. While the light of day surrounded her, she was trapped within perpetual night as darkness started to fill her thoughts. She was not much help to any of their missions, for there was little hope and light left within her. How could she conjure enough to destroy any more orbs when she felt a kinship with it, the same blackness that entered the soul just before it gave up everything that it was?

Lyssa spent her afternoon looking for signs of new portals forming in the world. There had been an increasing rate of portals, and while they had been taking the orbs down within the Land of Shadows, there was still a link between their worlds, as they had not actually successfully closed any of the portals. It seemed to be the next step, but in order to do that, they would need to rid their world of the Craven that kept opening them. Logically, they could take down every portal possible, but there was still the black magic of the Craven out there. They would only continue to cause a problem if the Watch Tower did not find a way to stop them. She kept reading and rereading any information that Logan and Hunter had collected.

It seemed to her that the Craven were somehow locking into some deeper black magic, and she was at a loss as to where it could possibly be coming from. Lyssa knew they had been mining the same rock materials that created the orbs in the Land of the Shadows, but there had to be some way that they were channeling energy from them. What exactly were they using? She made a note to ask Logan to search further for any keys that would help them…wands, crystals, orbs. There had to be something they were missing. It all had to start somewhere else.

That night when she went to bed, she expected sleep to elude her once more. Lyssa was surprised that her eyelids closed easily, and the sweet warm embrace of sleep pulled her deep under. Soon, she was dreaming about Hunter again. It was the only time she got to see him. Her dreams up until this point had been laced with memories of their blissful time together, making her wake up feeling even worse than when she went to sleep, for seeing him so real and alive made it hard to let go of the idea that he was still not gone. The others saw her light deteriorating right before them and tried to encourage her to move on.

Tonight her dreams were different. She saw Hunter within some kind of dark cave. His body was badly battered, but he was breathing steadily. His eyes opened, and it looked as if he had been unconscious for quite some time. His body was shackled to the ground with the black snakelike chains she had seen wrapped around the souls in the first portal, but he was not bodiless like the others. He was in full form and trapped within some place she did not recognize.

Her soul reached out to him across the void and whispered his name. *Hunter?*

Hunter looked around as if he were trying to catch a leaf on a breeze as her voice echoed in the cave around him. *Lyssa. I'm here.*

Is that really you? Lyssa could see the grimace he made as he tried to move to another position. He had been badly beaten, and his face was so swollen, it was almost hard to see the smile that tried to break across his lips.

I'm a little battered, but not broken.

I'll find you Hunter. If it is the last thing I do.

Lyssa woke suddenly and sat up, shaking. She tried to pull her thoughts together. Never had a dream felt so real before. She closed her eyes and willed her thoughts to slow down inside her. Lyssa tried not to cry out, because this dream had felt so real. But the biggest part of her was telling her that it couldn't be true.

Putting her hand on the locket she constantly wore around her neck, she prayed to the gods to feel his energy present. Lyssa sent her wishes quietly out into the air before trying to reach out to him with her mind. *Hunter?*

It took a few seconds for his voice to register through to her, but she heard the faint reply. *I'm here, Lyssa.*

We'll find you Hunter! Lyssa jumped out of the bed and teleported to the library as quickly as possible. She knew it was still early morning, but she didn't care. Running her fingers across the number 4 etched into her arm, she sent every ounce of energy into summoning the others. Lyssa called them a few times before the first of them made their way to the room. Finally, Serena and Julius made their way to the library, and it was clear that each one had just pulled themselves out of bed.

"What is it Lyssa?"

"It's Hunter."

Julius was trying hard not to roll aggravated eyes at her. "Look Lyssa, we told you."

"He's alive, Julius. He's been unconscious, but he just woke up. He is trapped within some dark cave, and my assumption is that he is trapped within one of the shadow portals. I'm thinking the Craven may have realized who he was. He's badly beaten, but he's alive. They're trying to break him."

"How do you know?"

"Come now, Julius. If anyone would know, it would be Lyssa. They're soul mates."

"Okay. So now what?" Julius looked over at her speculatively.

"Now we find Hunter. I'll start looking through my index of portals and see where I feel his presence the strongest. As long as he remains conscious, then I should be able to find him. We will need quite a few guardians to help get him out, and we will have to stake out the place before we attempt a rescue."

"Let me know if you need anything. I'll make sure you have any support you need. We will always fight for one of our own." Julius put his hand on her shoulder and patted her comfortingly. It was the first time Julius had offered her comfort since Hunter was taken.

"We have a lot of work to do, Julius. But rest assured, if there is anything you know to be true, it's this; I will not stop until we bring him home."

Elissa Daye

Chapter 31

Lyssa spent the next two days continuing to hop from portal to portal, returning to portals she'd already seen, visiting new ones that had never been entered, but she was having a difficult time tracking down Hunter. She knew his energy levels were low because he was in and out of consciousness, but she could still feel his presence.

Her dreams at night were filled with him, as somehow reaching her soul out to him seemed easier in the world of sleep. Lyssa could see the cave quite distinctly, the rugged edges of stone jutting out carelessly around him. Sometimes there were a few torches burning inside the cave, but when the light was burning, the shadows were missing. She could see members of the Craven taking their turns interrogating Hunter with their fists, chains, and belts. Lyssa woke up screaming many times, as her body took in the images that her soul was seeing. He was living hell every day, and yet the strength of his pure will kept him alive. They had to find him soon.

She sat at the globe in the library and held the locket in her right hand. Lyssa put her left hand on the globe and sent her mind to probe for his spirit. She kept waiting to feel his presence, but it was just not coming to her. Slamming her fist on the table, she dropped the locket onto the globe. Tears sprang to her eyes, for it was getting hard to hold them inside. Lyssa was losing faith in her ability to find him, and the whole prospect started to feel bleaker each day.

She watched as the locket was pulled along with the spinning globe. Lyssa went to grab it before it got caught between the wooden table and where the globe curved into it. As she reached for the locket, it raced across the globe in the opposite direction. She jumped out of her seat and watched closely as it zipped back and forth across the globe, almost as if some magnetic pull was powering it. Then suddenly, it stopped and stood straight up on one area of the globe, with the bottom of the locket touching the globe and the strands of the necklace streaming through the air, waving much like the tentacles of a jellyfish. She sat there transfixed by the moment, almost afraid to reach out and disturb the locket. Clearly, Hunter wanted her to find him, and somewhere inside her, she knew she had to find him as soon as possible.

Lyssa picked up the locket, placed it in her pocket and went to change into her dark clothing. She would scope out the area first, then she would ask the others to join her.

Lyssa closed her eyes, pictured the spot on the map, and moved quickly through the air. When her feet touched ground, she opened her eyes quickly. Running a finger over the locket, she imagined Hunter's face. Her only hope was that they would get to him fast enough. She took in the atmosphere around her. Lyssa was surrounded by hedges that were so tall she could not see over them. She put her hand out and touched them to see where they separated, but she could not tell where one hedge started and the other ended. From what she could tell, it seemed to be a hedge maze.

The locket was almost burning a hole through her pocket. She pulled it out, and Hunter's energy yanked on it, making her feel like she was walking an oversized dog. She followed the silvery leash as it led her around one corner then another. Soon, she was running through the maze, dodging branches protruding from some of the untended hedges and trying not to swallow dusty cobwebs. This maze was clearly not one that was used often. When she turned right, she could not only feel the portal, she could actually see it. This portal was definitely different from the others. It did not have the same shadow signature at all. This felt more like the Craven. It was easy to assume Hunter was being held in the Land of the Shadows, and if that were the case, her initial desire to scout it out by herself would simply not be logical. Lyssa had to go back to the Watch Tower to get the others. That's all there was to it.

After teleporting back, Lyssa called the other members of Sector 4. She had not expected to see Logan appear with the others, but this time he did, and his face was extremely nervous and agitated.

"Logan?"

Lyssa had not seen him in months, and he was definitely not the same man she had once known. Gone were the innocent locks framing his face. His hair now stood up like straight spikes from his head. The brown color was now a dark black with reddened tips. His unmarked face now held piercings that would never have fit him before. The others were looking at him too. It was unusual for him to conference with them. Most of his dealings with the Craven were reported to Julius, and then Julius would report his findings to them.

"Hunter is in danger. If you don't get to him as soon as humanly possible, they are going to make me kill him."

"If they can't get to him, you must keep your cover at all costs," Julius answered him quietly.

Lyssa felt as if a sentence had been handed down by a Superior Court Judge. It was so final. If she did not save Hunter today, he would be lost to her. She would never forgive Julius if they did not get to him fast enough. "What the hell? Seriously? How could you say that? All life is important, Julius. If we knowingly let him die, we are breaking our own directive, and I might add that makes us no better than the darkness we are fighting against."

"Don't worry, Lyssa. I wouldn't let that happen anyway. If I have to break my cover I will, but I am definitely going to need back up as soon as possible."

"Then we better do everything we can now." It came out more like a threat than anything else. They did not want to deal with her if they let Hunter die.

"He's being guarded by a handful of shadows and a dozen Craven. You will need to bring reinforcements. Unfortunately, I can't stay here. If I do, then they will know I had something to do with your arrival." They all nodded to Logan before he teleported from the room.

"Let's summon some of the others and get this moving then." Julius looked over at her with at least an ounce of regret for his decisions.

Lyssa nodded at him. "I know where the portal is. Hunter has been leading me to it today. He must know what's going on around him. We'll have to go as soon as we can."

Julius quickly flipped a switch from the table, and the television screen came down from the ceiling. He pushed a few buttons, and they were now looking at four different panels in the screen. Each panel held the communications room from another sector of the Watch Tower.

"We need help rescuing Hunter. It won't be an easy fight, but if we don't go as soon as possible, his life will be forfeit."

"Here is where the portal is located." Lyssa pointed to the spot the locket had marked on the map. "We'll have to go through a maze to get through the portal. I can lead the way. We'll need to leave at once."

"Do you have your jump point?" Julius asked them, and when they all nodded in affirmation, he nodded his head. "Let's move out."

Their wands were already drawn as they teleported away from the Watch Tower. Close to twenty guardians stood at the entrance of the maze. She let the locket lead her, much as before, and they started their chase through the maze. When they reached the portal, she put her hand up. "We should go in a few at a time."

Lyssa walked through the portal and was instantly whisked away to a new destination. She felt her feet hit the ground and stepped to the side quickly to allow for anyone else to enter while she quickly took in her surroundings. There were stone walls in every direction…some behind her, in front of her to each side, and when she looked up, she even saw the sky was lined with endless walls. This was so much more than the maze they had exited…this was a world filled with the twisted walls of a labyrinth that was going to be a nightmare to get through. She felt the energy around her covered in a murky warning that something dangerous could happen at any corner, and it made it all that more real to her. Hunter was definitely in danger.

When all of them were finally through the portal, Julius turned to the group. "I know you are thinking that we might have better odds of getting through this if we split up, but I think we are better served if we stay together."

"Do you think they're expecting us?" asked Serena.

"I think we should assume anything is possible at this point," he answered.

"He's right. Safety in numbers. You never know what might be around the corner." Lyssa felt the locket's energy vibrate in her hand. She held onto the clasp and waited for it to direct them through to Hunter. If she had to guess, this labyrinth was going to take some effort to get through. If they had already known the terrain, teleporting closer to Hunter would be no problem, but without that knowledge teleporting to him could be disastrous.

They walked in silence, but the eerie quiet surrounding them did not make her feel safe at all. The quiet was anything but serene and did nothing to calm the nerves racing through her body. She followed the locket's pull from corner to corner, and when she made the next turn, she heard a screech like she had never heard before. Lyssa stopped in her tracks and peered just around the corner. The path was covered in animated, statuesque beings. She could not tell what they were because they were still quite a distance away. She gestured to the others to take a peek and waited for a group consensus.

"We have no idea what those things will do to us."

When it sounded like the group would be gridlocked until someone volunteered to find out, she stuck her chin out defiantly. "Fine. You wait here. I'll figure it out then. Hunter's life is in the balance."

She teleported right in front of the beings and immediately cast an energy shield around her. The statues turned to face her, and she was staring into the face of a stone gargoyle with fangs that were moving menacingly in her direction. The stone creaked as the gargoyle stretched its wings.

When light started to fill its eyes to a haunting green glow, she knew she was about to be attacked. As it rose in the air, the stone keeping it in its place cracked into chunks that now rolled on the ground. The heavy wings rose and fell in the air, making large whooshing sounds. The green light shot forth from its eyes like a laser, and she raised her wand to deflect it. The rays ricocheted into the wall to her right and seared a hole through the cement.

When it tried to attack her with its eyes one more time, blast after blast of light flew past her ears at it. She ducked her head to give the guardians room to attack, while sending a few of her own blasts at it. It exploded into dust in front of her, and she took a deep breath of relief. Lyssa couldn't help feeling that this had been cutting it a little close, but she saw Hunter's face in her mind, and she knew that they had to push on.

When she walked another few feet, she heard more rustling to her left side. When she looked up, there were five more gargoyles flapping their leaden wings as they flew noisily towards them. She ducked as green flashes of light shot at her, and teleported back to where the rest of her group was standing. She felt a red hot sting on her arm, and when she looked down she could see where one of the gargoyles had just barely hit her with their beam. She shrugged off the pain and continued to send every bit of energy she could at them. Another guardian doubled over in pain as a blast seared through her shoulder, but she, too, continued to fight through the pain, until finally every gargoyle had been obliterated into ash in front of them.

Lyssa ripped off a piece of her shirt and tied it around her wound. She was not going to let it slow her down. The guardian who had been hit was losing a lot of blood.

"You should go back. You're no good to us if we have to worry about you." Julius put a hand on her shoulder, and she nodded in agreement before teleporting away. "We move."

Lyssa held the locket out once again and mentally pleaded for it to lead her to Hunter. She felt the same pull she had before and continued to follow wherever it was leading her. She walked at least another mile before she felt the tugging chain start to pull twice as hard and then fall. "We can't wait anymore. I'm teleporting."

"Wait Lyssa. You don't know where you're going."

"I don't care, Julius. We're running out of time. His energy is getting weaker every minute we walk through this mess."

"Yes, but you'll be putting him at risk. Logan said we had some time. We'll get there."

"I'm going, Julius."

"I forbid it, Lyssa. Your life is just as important. And it's what Hunter would want too."

"Screw that!" Lyssa moved through air before Julius could stop her and landed on the edge of an opening. She sent a message to them telling what she saw. *"There are twelve guards and eight shadows surrounding Hunter. Logan is there, and he is carrying an athame over to Hunter. Come to me, and hurry!"*

The Craven guarding Hunter detected the guardians as soon as they teleported next to her, and started to attack them. The guardians retaliated in kind. Blast after blast of energy was thrown towards the Craven standing in front of Hunter. The tallest man turned to Logan. "Kill him, now!" Logan barely looked in their direction as he raised his hands with the athame over Hunter's head.

"No!" The scream came from the most horrified part of her. Lyssa knew that Logan would not attack him, but she could not guarantee that the man standing next to him wouldn't. She sailed through the air faster than she ever had and crouched down by Hunter's side just moments before the blade came down toward him. Lyssa saw Hunter wish her away, but she refused to budge. Her shield was up so fast the blade did not have a chance to reach either of them. It bounced off it and she raised her wand, firing off a bolt of light that sent Logan reeling. She knew she had not sent enough at him to kill him, but she had sent enough energy so as not to make them suspicious of his connection to the Watch Tower. Lyssa held onto Hunter and continued to shield him as the guardians made their best attempt at taking down the shadows and Craven swarming around them.

Four of the guardians were seriously injured before the Craven ducked out of sight, but they had taken out at least half of the group that had been left watching Hunter. Lyssa watched as the others kneeled in front of their wounded while she tried to help Hunter to his feet. He grimaced in pain as she touched a bruised rib, but he managed to smile at her just the same. They stood around the black orb that was just barely breaking the surface of the ground. It took them an instant to shatter it between them, and then the world around them was finally at peace. As soon as the smoke settled, they started teleporting away.

Elissa Daye

Chapter 32

After getting Hunter settled into their hospital wing at the Watch Tower, she made her way back to their library. Julius was sitting there with several other guardians. Lyssa cleared her throat as she entered the room.

"Lyssa. Join us, please."

"Of course." She sat down at the table and tried not to look uncomfortable. Lyssa felt bad that some of the guardians had been injured on their mission to save Hunter.

"They have been telling me about their findings from one of the portals you've located. You will be interested to hear what they have found."

Lyssa turned to face the others and gave them her closest attention. "Please do tell."

Rodger, an older guardian, was the first to answer. "When we entered the portal, we were surprised to find the world was very simple. We were let out above a ridge that overlooked a huge clearing that reminded me vaguely of an empty battlefield. In the center of the clearing was an encampment of Craven and shadows who were guarding the largest orb we have seen to date."

"This orb was different from the others," Jacob added. "It was clear, almost like a glass bead, and a black smoky substance was floating around in it. As we watched, the shadows extracted some of this material from it. It streamed through the air and began to circle around quickly before forming orbs that we can only assume are the obsidian orbs that we have been destroying."

"If what you are telling me is accurate, I would feel comfortable saying that this orb could be the source of their power," interrupted Julius.

"You think this orb may be behind the powers of both the shadows and the Craven?" Lyssa looked at Julius. It was possible that by destroying this orb, there was a very good chance that they could defeat these two powers once and for all. She pursed her lips in concentration as she was running various scenarios of outcomes through her head. "If this is the case, you can bet that more Craven and shadows will be summoned the moment our people attack. They would need the full force of the Watch Tower behind them."

"Okay, so when do we attack?"

"First we will need to organize our attack. We'll need to counsel with the leaders of the Watch Tower."

"We need to be quick, Julius. They are surely working out other ways to attack our world. If we don't take care of this situation soon, it will be more difficult to manage," Rodger added to the conversation.

More difficult to manage? Had they actually been managing anything? Every time they destroyed one orb, another came swiftly in its place. A new portal, a new passage to the Land of Shadows rose swiftly from the ground. They had to get a handle on this situation if they were to wipe away the misery that haunted the people of their world.

It was hard to agree yet disagree at the same time. Yes, she felt like they needed to attack as soon as possible, but as with anything else they had done to this point, it was entirely possible that they were already in preparation for an attack. This was not going to be an easy feat. There was a drive in her that wanted to rush through this process too, but in doing so, would the outcome be what they wanted it to be? This should be something that was thought out. There could be repercussions. People may be lost. She wanted to voice all these concerns, but she knew they would be talking about these things with the others.

Lyssa went to go see Hunter after they had left. She wanted to tell him what she had just learned, but a part of her said now was not the time. More than likely, he would want to jump into the fray, and she had no idea what the outcome would be with him already being banged up and bruised. When she entered his room, his eyes opened. He smiled as much as his battered face would allow him. "Lyssa."

"Hunter." She smiled softly at him and reached over to touch his hand. "I never gave up."

"I knew you wouldn't."

"It looks like you're going to be on the mend here soon." It was polite talk. She didn't want to tell him about what was on the verge of happening. Lyssa wanted to keep the danger of their pursuits hidden from him. He would need to focus on his recovery. If she told him too much, she knew he would drag himself out of that bed.

"I'm okay, Lyssa. I'll heal." He raised his hand to her cheek, and she was pulled back to a time and place friendlier than the present, when their bodies were one, and the heat between them kept them warm from the cold. She could feel her lips turning up into a smile automatically. "So what's going on?"

"I'm sorry? What do you mean?"

"Well, there has to be a reason you have your thoughts on lock down, Lyssa. What happened?"

She sighed deeply. Lyssa knew Hunter would not rest until he knew what had happened, but she felt like he should be protected from this moment. He had just gotten back from such a horrible mess. "I don't think you need to know right now, Hunter."

"You know I'll find out; why don't you just tell me?" His smile was quickly turning to a frown.

"I don't know what to tell you, Hunter. We have found something that could be the power source of the Craven and the shadows. We're going to destroy it." That was simple enough. She did not need to tell him the whole kit and caboodle.

"Lyssa, if that were the only thing on your mind, you would've just told me. There has to be more."

Lyssa looked away from him and took another breath. How could she expect him to let go of this if she would be as adamant? "It could be dangerous, the biggest fight the Watch Tower has ever seen, but we're not going to rush into it. We'll go when we have an organized plan of attack."

"When?"

"I don't know, Hunter, but I expect it will be before you recover."

"I'm going with you." One simple statement, and her head was reeling, her heart pounding. She would not be effective in any battle if she had to worry about Hunter.

"No, you're not," came a stiff voice from the door. Julius was standing there glaring at Hunter.

"That's what I was trying to tell him. Maybe he'll listen to you." Lyssa stood up briskly and was about to leave the room when Hunter interrupted her departure.

"Fine. But you'd better make sure she gets back to me."

She turned back in time to hear Julius reply, "You have my word."

Chapter 33

It had been decided that they were going to attack at dawn three days later. The leaders had organized them enough that they could move through the portal in waves that would allow them to spread out along the ridge. They knew that as soon as they entered the portal with such force that other Craven and shadows would be entering the portal behind them, so the timing of their entry had to be swift. The past two days had been spent taking turns monitoring the ridge at different times. A large group was always surrounding the orb, so there had to be some truth to their assumptions about its origins.

Today was the day, and her thoughts were running rampant. Today could be the end of the shadows on Earth, no more darkness covering the hearts and homes of the people she loved. Their world would be a much healthier place. Lyssa looked forward to putting a stop to the evil that fed on the weakness and despair of others.

Following Julius through the portal, she was not surprised to see Jackson standing beside the other guardians who had already lined up around the portal. Lyssa raced over to his side and threw her arms around him. "I missed you!"

"Of course you did." Jackson gave her a smirk and hugged her back.

"There's so much—"

"No time for that right now." Jackson stepped away from her and looked around at the others.

"Right. For Lana?"

"For Lana."

They both walked over to the where the first line stood. A heavy ridge about a mile in radius circled the clearing. Stones staggered like bricks were held together with the mortar of earth around hugging them, making the sides of the ridge appear more like a gentle mountain. Tree lines surrounded the base of the ridge, providing quite the cover for enemy attackers. The roads cutting through the clearing were covered in shadows and Craven, all crouching over the largest orb she had ever seen. This was the main source of all their power. By destroying this orb, they could take out the Craven and shadows at the same time; but first they would have to deal with the entities blocking their path to the orb and any beings that came through the portal behind them.

The guardians were dividing up as they came through the portal: those that took the front line and those that guarded their backs. It didn't take long for the shadows to notice the movement on the ridge. It was almost as if they were anticipating an attack.

A large whistle echoed around the guardians, their signal to start creating a ball of light big enough to send to the orb in the middle. It started small like a soccer ball, then grew almost as if air was being pushed into it. Soon it was the size of a hot air balloon and rose in the air with all the might in their hearts. They lifted up every hopeful feeling and every loving memory of the world they knew and pushed it forward. The ball of light now sparkled like a disco ball as rays of rainbow colored light filtered into the world around them. When the orb was as large as their power could hold, they sent it flying towards the orb in the middle. Shadows and Craven sent black bolts of light at the orb as it hurtled to the middle of the clearing, but to no avail. The guardians used the strength of the Watch Tower, set up centuries before to protect their world, and they were not going to be stopped now.

The ball flew into the black orb, like a bubble hitting the ground slowly. When it attached itself to the orb, she watched in amazement, because she had assumed it would shatter the orb into tiny little pieces, but that was not what happened at all. Their light started to swallow the dark orb whole, and its entirety could be seen within it. Little by little, the darkness siphoned out of the orb, and each little trickle of blackness was being extinguished inside. When all of the blackness disappeared, no orb remained inside. The ball of light that they had created rose into the air, where it exploded tiny droplets of light onto the world below them.

It was then that the shadows and Craven charged at them. It was a desperate attempt to overpower the Watch Tower. The droves coming through the portal were proof that their assumptions were right. The world around them was a mess in minutes. Shadows jumped the ridge while Craven teleported at them. Wands were flashing lights in every direction. Animal spirits, totems they all held dear, were running around fighting at the heels of their attackers. People were falling all around them, and it was not clear as to who would survive this battle.

A shadow jumped in front of her as she was about to attack the Craven firing on Jackson. She jabbed the hot end of her wand into its belly and ripped a hole right through it. It shrieked horribly in her ear, but she sent all the energy she could into it. Its dark body imploded from the light she had sent within.

When it had been obliterated, she went for her next target, the Craven who had been attacking Jackson. Jackson had been doing a decent job defending himself from him, but he did not see the Craven teleport in behind him, who raised a sword in the air and started to swing it at Jackson. "Jackson, duck!"

When he ducked, she launched an arrow of light from her wand. The dark haired Craven fell when the arrow pierced through his chest. She turned away, knowing that Jackson would be okay. Three more shadows advanced toward her, and she conjured a net in her hands. She swung the ropes swiftly through the air and threw it around them as they tried to pounce on her. Lyssa pulled the net tight and watched as the shadows exploded into dust underneath its bright light.

She felt a blade slice through her arm and turned around to see another Craven to her left. He had tried to attack another guardian near her and had hit her in the process. They were all standing so close to each other, it was hard to make heads or tails of anything. Lyssa put a hand over her injury and raised the wand in her other. She continued to lance ball after ball of light at the shadows around them, since attacking the shadows had almost become second nature to her.

The battle lasted for hours, wand to sword, light to dark. Each side was losing energy, but it was clear that there would be a victor this day, and when the Craven started to teleport away from the battle, they knew that rest would soon be at hand. Lyssa had lost sight of the rest of Sector 4 amidst the chaos, but as she looked around she could see that they were all still fighting. The guardians continued to take down the shadows that circled them, but as time wore on, these beings started to retreat as well. When they stood among only guardians, they took stock of the situation.

Lyssa looked at the bodies on the ground around them. There were many casualties that day, as they knew there would be. The fear of death was not nearly as great as the fear that darkness would be the only thing that their world would ever know. Those that had died had not died in vain. They had sacrificed their lives so that others might know a better way. Each and every one of them had entered this day knowing it might be their last. They took a long moment to pay respect to those that had passed among them before moving them along to the eternal slumber that was their just reward.

While others returned quickly to the Watch Tower, Lyssa took her time. Jackson and Lyssa both assisted with the bodies of their friends and colleagues. It was important to them that they helped send them to a better place, considering the immeasurable gift the guardians had given to their world. When they had finished, both of them embraced one last time, knowing that they would touch base with each other as soon as possible.

Lyssa returned to the Watch Tower the next morning. It was time to see the only thing that mattered to her now that her purpose as a guardian had been fulfilled.

When she entered his room, Hunter almost stood up from his bed, and looked as if he had seen a ghost. "Stay," she ordered him. She walked over to his bed and put her hand in his. It was clear that he had been sitting there contemplating the worst.

"They said there had been casualties. My powers were too weak to find you, and when you didn't return with the others, I thought—"

"That I was one of them? No. As you can see, I made it through just fine. I'm sorry you worried, but I had to help move our fallen friends on to the next life. It was the right thing to do, considering I still had so much more left of mine."

"So what happens next?"

"I assume the guardians will start tearing down the portals for safe measure. We can't be too careful where the shadows and Craven are concerned. Not all of them were destroyed, but we did take out the major power source."

"And?"

"I'm sorry, what?" She had been distracted by thoughts of the aftermath. Lyssa looked over at Hunter.

"And what else?"

She couldn't help the smirk she knew filled her face. "What else was there again? First we infiltrated the Craven, tracked the shadows, and annihilated the orbs. We'll remove the portals, and then…I'm sorry, was there something else?" She knew she was teasing him, but she could not resist.

"Come here!" He pulled her into his lap so quickly that she almost fell off the bed laughing. It felt right to laugh, even with the hardship that had just passed through the Watch Tower. None of those that had gone before them would want them to live in regret or sorrow for their lives. They would want them to live, love, laugh, and be happy. That she was sure of, because today was a brand new day, and it was filled with endless possibilities. Starting with a kiss and ending with whatever else dared to follow.

About the Author

Ever since childhood, Elissa Daye has enjoyed reading stories as an escape from life. When she was a teenager she started to write her own stories that kept her entertained when she ran out of books to read. When she was accepted into Illinois Summer School for the Arts in her Junior year of High School, she knew she wanted to become a writer. Elissa graduated from Illinois State University in December 1999 with a Bachelor of Science in Elementary Education and began her teaching career, hoping to find moments to write in her free time.

After seven years of teaching, Elissa decided to focus on her writing and made the decision to put her teaching years behind her so that she could create the stories she had always dreamed of. She is now happily married and a stay at home mom, who writes in every spare moment she can find, doing her best to master the art of multitasking to get everything accomplished.

Made in the USA
Middletown, DE
18 May 2015